Dr. Crawford paused momentarily before speaking. "Jim, we only have a few minutes, and I will do my best to explain our mission as succinctly as possible. . . . At this point, suffice it to say that we feel we are on the verge of the most significant biblical discovery of all times." He paused to scan the faces around the table.

**"We think we're about to secure a manuscript of the Gospel of Luke—in Luke's own handwriting!"**

*Bibl Fict,*

_Andrew Jenkins_

# THE MANUSCRIPT

# DONALD C. KING

**LIVING BOOKS**
Tyndale House Publishers, Inc.
Wheaton, Illinois

First printing, September 1984

Library of Congress Catalog Card Number 84-50855
ISBN 0-8423-3901-9, Living Books edition
Copyright © 1984 by Donald C. King
Printed in the United States of America

*To Lynne*
*wife,*
*lover,*
*typist,*
*best friend*

## ACKNOWLEDGMENTS

*The Manuscript,* as any historical novel, contains both real and imaginary characters. I have tried to portray the real persons (biblical and historical) in a manner consistent with their character—that is, I have had them say and do things they *could* have done (in my opinion at least), based on what we know about them from the historical record.

A few books should be noted as being especially helpful in the research for this story: *Paul the Traveller* by Ernie Bradford is a well-written account of first-century navigation of the Mediterannean; *A Visit to Monasteries in the Levant,* a minor classic by Robert Curzon first published in 1849, was helpful in portraying monastic life in the nineteenth century; also I must acknowledge the influence of William H. McNeill's *Plagues and Peoples,* on the impact of infectious diseases on world history.

I would also like to thank Southeastern Bible College Library, the Vestavia Hills Library, and the Birmingham Library (particularly the interlibrary loan department) for their assistance in my research.

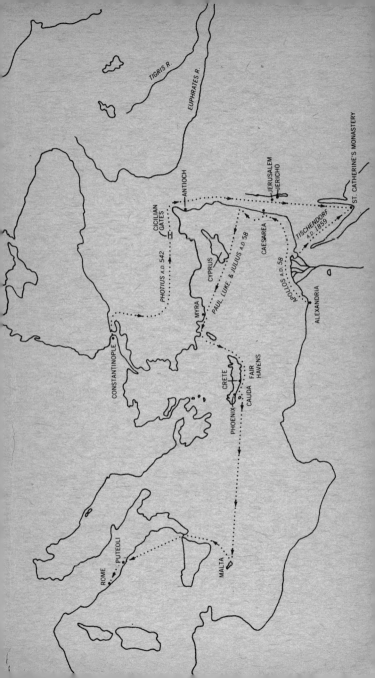

# 1

"No, Alex, the answer is a firm no."

Jim Matthews was speaking from a poolside phone in St. Thomas. The puddle of water forming around his feet glistened in the tropical sun. The hotel was high above the bay and commanded a view of dozens of small sailboats that dotted the smooth blue waters of the famous harbor. Beyond the neck of the harbor a glittering white cruise ship was making a late-morning departure into the deeper waters on its way to some other Caribbean port, its occupants heavily laden with cigarettes, liquor, jewelry and other items from the celebrated free port.

"Alex, I told you I was taking some time off—I'm not interested in your assignment. I'm tired. I intend to sleep twelve hours each night and nap by the pool all day. I intend to interrupt that routine only often enough to take periodic hot showers—in the hope of eventually washing that Brazilian jungle out of my skin."

The voice on the other end of the line was that of Alexander Adams, publisher of *Monitor* magazine. "Jim, I appreciate your need to rest. You've been going hard for several months, but. . . ."

"Good, then we're agreed. Call me again in two weeks. I should be restored to my health by then and you should have all those rolls of film developed and edited and. . . ."

"They're already developed," Alex answered. "They were on my desk when I came in this morning—they're good."

"*Good?*" Jim retorted. His raised voice aroused nearby sunbathers from their slumber and they turned in his direction. Jim turned his back to them and cupped the phone to his mouth. "Listen Alex, do you have any idea what it's like to spend seventeen days in the Brazilian interior? Do you know how it feels to backpack with four cameras, a dozen lenses, and assorted other paraphenalia when the temperature and humidity total two hundred? And sleeping every night with all that gear chained to your body so it won't be stolen? And Alex, that insect repellant you sent—the local mosquitoes thought it was booze—they lapped it up. And leeches—do you want to hear about the leeches, Alex?"

"Jim, calm down, the pictures are magnificent. They always are. I didn't mean to hurt your feelings. Besides, you should be proud of yourself. When these pictures hit the newsstand, it should bring some pressure on the Brazilian government to enact some measures to protect the Indians from those lumber companies."

"Frankly Alex, I'm just too tired right now to feel like a real humanitarian. I'm tired and I'm a little edgy—which is all the more reason I'm not interested in your assignment. I need some time to unwind. I'll fly to New York in a week or ten days. Then we'll sit down and plan the whole thing."

"A week will be too late, Jim. Two days may be too late. This one won't wait. It's a big one, Jim, a real big one."

"Don't tell me another war is breaking out. I really don't feel up to a war right now. I've taken enough pictures of corpses to last a lifetime."

"No, Jim, it's not a war."

"Well, what is it then?"

"I can't talk about it now, Jim. But there's a ticket waiting for you at the airport. Your flight leaves at 4:15. You'll be in New York before midnight. I'll have someone meet you and you can sleep in my office. I'll see you early in the morning."

"But Alex. . . ."

"Really, Jim, I need you badly for this one. Early in the morning, OK?"

There was a pause as Jim turned and surveyed the scene around him. A waiter efficiently went about his task of removing the empty plastic cups that cluttered the tables around the pool. An older couple examined their morning's purchases around a canopied table. A long-limbed young woman lay nearby in a bikini, her nose and lips covered with thick cream, startlingly white against her oily-brown body. Beyond the bay the cruise

13

steered between some of the small outer islands, extravagantly green in the midday sun.

"Jim, are you still there?" Alex's voice came over the phone.

"Yeah, I'm here." He heard the flatness in his own voice.

"First thing in the morning?"

"Well . . . I don't know why . . . but—I guess. First thing in the morning. . . ."

He'd given in again.

Jim put the phone down in slow motion. Methodically he began to gather his possessions from the small table beside his lounge chair. He made his way toward the lobby. He stopped abruptly in front of the glass door when he saw his reflection in the brilliant sunshine. Except for his shoulders, which seemed somewhat weary, his body seemed to belong to someone younger than his thirty-two years. But it was the expression on his face that had arrested his attention—the expression of a man about to ask a question. He took one step toward the glass as if he were going to examine his reflection more closely, but a tour group pushed open the door and a squatty little lady in a straw hat with a camera around her neck looked at him strangely, so he smiled politely and went on into the lobby. "That jungle has done strange things to me," he mumbled to himself as he made his way to his room.

As he packed, Jim noticed the business cards Alex had given him. "James Matthews, Photo-Journalist" they said. That was more than a little presumptuous, he thought, and

the box was still completely full. Jim knew he
was not a journalist—he hardly ever wrote a
complete sentence. The most he'd written was
captions to accompany his photographs:
"Starving Biafran children being fed by Red
Cross" or "Bodies of rebels litter the street
where government and insurgents fought a
bloody two-hour battle earlier in the day."

Jim knew he was no journalist. His was a
stricter medium of communication—one which
allowed for less subjectivity. He was a photog-
rapher.

However it still amazed him to write "pho-
tographer" on one of the blank lines of the
endless government papers he endured as he
traveled. He had never pressed the shutter
release of a camera until he was nearly
twenty-three years old. A college dropout in
the middle of his second year, he worked with
a road construction crew several months
before he was drafted.

Soon he found himself on another stretch of
highway, one less than a mile long, surrounded by the dense Asian jungle. There it
was his job each morning to load napalm and
machine gun rounds on the F-4's and F-105's
that daily screamed down the blacktop, silently lifting off at the end of the runway banking
over the lush green jungle.

Jim conditioned himself not to think about
the napalm or the ammunition, or even the
planes and pilots that sometimes did not
return. He had bought a calendar the first day
he arrived in Vietnam, and circling his release
date eleven months in the future, he taped it
inside his locker. Every night before he went

to bed, he dutifully crossed the day off the
calendar. Load napalm in the morning. Cross
the day off at night. That was his routine.

The calendar had a different picture for each
month: a view of the Swiss Alps one month; a
scene of mown wheat in Kansas another;
Buckingham Palace once; and a stream in the
Rockies after that. The pictures were glossy
and beautiful and on the first day of the
month he would often stare in admiration for
some minutes.

But he never allowed himself to turn the
page to look ahead. His system was simple:
load in the morning, cross the day off at
night.

Usually the war stayed away from the
blacktop strip in the jungle. The war was a
separate place, a separate reality.

Occasionally, however, the war would in-
trude.

The first instance came when Jim had been
there only a few weeks. They had all watched
as a plane wobbled toward the clearing; black
smoke billowing behind, leaving an erratic
trail in the sky. The plane hit hard, and slid
off the runway, but it did not explode.

Jim was one of the first to reach the plane
and as he helped to tear the canopy off, he
could smell the sweet, putrid odor of blood
mixed with oil. The pilot's right leg had been
torn away by the surface-to-air missile, but he
had retained consciousness long enough to
bring the plane back.

That night Jim opened his locker and looked
at the calendar. He wished he could keep the
war away, but he couldn't. Like a recurring
dream, it always crept back when it wasn't ex-

pected. Its odor and essence were present in that place. He dutifully marked the day off with a neat X, one of a long series on the page.

Load ammunition in the morning; cross the day off at night—that was his routine, his liturgy.

He bought the Nikkormat from a GI trying to settle some gambling debts. He hadn't really wanted it, but the kid persisted, and after all, fifty dollars was only one-third its worth in Japan, and it would have retailed for well over two hundred dollars stateside.

Nonetheless, Jim kept the camera in his locker for more than a week before trying it out. After he learned how to operate it, he took it to the runway one day where he snapped a picture of a fresh-faced young pilot emerging from the cockpit of an F-4 after his first combat mission—he was flashing a huge smile and a thumbs-up sign.

That photograph and the wide smile of the green young pilot communicated a sense of enthusiasm. *Pathetic enthusiasm,* Jim thought in retrospect. *No one ever mentioned that the young pilot never returned from his second mission.* But the observer was captured immediately by the picture. It was a flashback to the heroes of World War II, where issues were more clear-cut, and heroes more abundant.

The chain of events that followed continued to amaze Jim for years afterward. His bunkmate pinned the photo to the barracks bulletin board; a UPI correspondent saw it and asked to use it. Soon the photo appeared in hundreds of U.S. newspapers, and Jim got a check for $200 in the mail. He promptly bought a couple of lenses and soon he was a regular contributor to several stateside publications.

Jim arrived at the airport in plenty of time to catch his 4:15 flight. The ticket was waiting for him just as Alex had promised. There was a telegraph as well:

JIM
THANKS STOP I APPRECIATE IT STOP YOU WON'T BE SORRY STOP DETAILS IN THE MORNING STOP
ALEX

Jim managed a smile. *You don't miss a lick, do you Alex?* he said to himself.

Soon he was aboard the DC-10 and above the shimmering Caribbean. As the plane droned over the water below, Jim had to admit to himself that he wasn't sorry he was going on this assignment, and he was more than a little bit curious about its secrecy. He *was* tired, but he wasn't sure two weeks in the Virgin Islands or anywhere else would help him. He recognized his symptoms—he had admitted it to himself weeks earlier—he had battle fatigue. He was able to diagnose it— hadn't he photographed it dozens of times on the faces of those suffering from it in Vietnam and elsewhere? The blurred eyes, the lax jaws, the insensitivity to outside stimuli—he had seen the same look in the face of an anesthetized tiger in Malaysia, with dull uncomprehending eyes and limp tongue hanging from his mouth.

Jim recalled a previous conversation with

Alex when he was being sent to South Africa to cover the race riots: "For goodness' sake, Alex, when is it going to stop? I go from riot to war to famine to tragedy; and then repeat the circuit—not necessarily in that order. How about a nice spread on a Sunday school outing? Or a 4-H convention? Or just a day in the park? Why does it have to be a variation of some form of gore to make your magazine? I can see the spread now. . . . 'Editor's note: Jim Matthews is providing Kodacolor prints (rich, red hues) of African blood this month. Next month we hope to have some shots of South American blood. Subsequent issues will feature carnage from other continents.' "

Jim's mind drifted back to the circumstances that brought him to where he was today. . . . *One dumb photograph,* he thought.

He found himself playing "what if?" more often these days: *What if the kid hadn't lost that poker hand; but had drawn the card he needed? What if he had sold a radio or cassette player instead of a camera? What if I hadn't taken the camera to the runway? What if the young pilot hadn't smiled?*

The possibilities were endless. It was a fruitless exercise. He fell asleep.

Alex was shaking Jim. "Wake up, wake up."

Jim awoke in Alex's office—rather in the bedroom of his office more than twenty stories above the ground. Jim could hardly remember the plane's arrival in New York or the ride to the office—those events had fused into a very ludicrous but realistic dream about a giant python eating all of his cameras.

"Your breakfast will be up in a few

minutes," Alex said. "It's good to see you again."

Jim glanced at his watch. "Seven o'clock! Are you kidding me?"

"You have just enough time to shave and take a quick shower. I have a couple of phone calls to make and I'll be right. . . ."

"*Phone calls!* Alex, it's seven o'clock in the morning! Since when did you start making calls at seven in the morning?"

"Oh Jim, I am so glad you've returned to brighten things up with your cheerful disposition—it's seven o'clock here but it's midafternoon in Israel. Take your shower. I'll be right back."

When Jim emerged from the shower, an elegant breakfast was waiting for him. The serving pieces bore the name of a swank hotel across the street. "I'm sure making deliveries isn't hotel policy," Jim muttered to himself.

He stuffed a buttered roll into his mouth. He could barely hear Alex on the phone in the next room: "Good, very good. Yes, they will be there late tomorrow morning."

"Tomorrow morning!" Jim shouted.

"Yes, tomorrow morning," Alex shouted back. "Now hurry up and eat your breakfast. We have company coming."

Jim stepped out into the outer office, his towel still wrapped around his waist. "Now just a doggone minute, Mr. Magazine Publisher. If you think you're going to drag me halfway around the world to take pictures for you when I don't even know what's. . . ."

There was a knock at the door.

"Oh good, that must be our guests. May I

suggest you put on your clothes? Miss Crawford might not appreciate your immodesty."

Jim ducked back into the little bedroom. He dressed quickly, came out, and Alex made the introductions.

"Dr. Crawford, Sarah, this is Jim Matthews, whom I've told you about. Jim, this is Dr. Enoch Crawford of the American Archaeological Institute and his niece, Sarah."

Dr. Crawford offered a vigorous handshake. Jim guessed he was in his mid-fifties. He was not tall, but there was strength in his features, accented by a deep tan and white-streaked hair.

"Glad to meet you, Jim. We've admired your work for several years, and Alex has told us a great deal about you."

Ordinarily Jim was uncomfortable around academic people—perhaps because he had never gotten a degree. But he found himself attracted to this man—the handshake, the genuine smile, the active, intelligent eyes. They all contributed to an extremely pleasant countenance.

"I must warn you, Jim," Dr. Crawford continued, "Sarah is more than my niece—she's the real brains of our expeditions. For the past two and a half years, she has been in charge of the administration of all our digs. And, I might add, she's the best in the business."

Sarah Crawford extended her hand to Jim. She was as tall as her uncle, with only a trace of makeup on her deeply tanned face. Her brown, sun-streaked hair was tied simply, but graciously, behind her head. *All in all*, Jim thought, *a very attractive young woman*.

"You must excuse my Uncle Enoch," she said. "He has no children or grandchildren to brag about, so he must use me."

"Not so, my dear. If I had had you to get me organized years ago, there's no telling how much more effective and fruitful our digging would have been."

"I'm sorry to break this up," Alex interrupted, "but the three of you had better get going. Jim, I've bought you a suitcase full of appropriate clothing. It's in the car already. Also there's a generous supply of film included. If you need any exotic lenses or particular tools, let me know and I'll have them delivered. There is cash waiting for you in Tel Aviv. If any other. . . ."

"Now just a doggone minute, Alex!" Jim broke in. "I'm not some kindergarten kid you can call in, wipe my nose, and send me out to play. Don't you think I have the right to know what's going on here? After all, yesterday afternoon I was beginning a well-deserved vacation when you snatched me away from the pool! And I think. . . ."

"OK, OK, Jim. Calm down," Alex said. He turned to Dr. Crawford. "It's up to you."

The archaeologist paced across the room with his head down. He turned to Alex. "Do you have a place where we could sit? I think Mr. Matthews is correct; he deserves an explanation."

When they had seated themselves in the conference room, Dr. Crawford opened the conversation. "Jim, please forgive us for our presumptuousness. I'm afraid, in our excitement, we completely ignored your feelings."

Jim started to mutter a "that's all right" but

22

Dr. Crawford silenced him with his hand.

"There is no excuse for running roughshod over people's feelings and demonstrating such glaring insensitivity. Will you forgive me?"

Jim felt like a fool. There was no question in his mind he was going on this assignment—any possible reservations about taking the job were removed when he met Sarah. A few weeks anywhere with her could hardly be considered a hardship. But he had indulged himself in a little tirade—a little temper tantrum—and now this archaeologist had his deep-set blue eyes riveted on him in absolute sincerity, asking forgiveness!

"Hey, it's no big deal. I just. . . ."

"No, I am asking," Dr. Crawford interrupted, "will you forgive me?"

"Certainly, I. . . ."

"Good. I hope to prove a more sensitive person in the future. That is, assuming you will be working with us in the future."

Jim noticed Alex out of the corner of his eye. He seemed to enjoy watching him squirm. He made a mental note to be careful what he said around the professor in the future.

Dr. Crawford paused momentarily before speaking. "Jim, we only have a few minutes, and I will do my best to explain our mission as succinctly as possible. If you accept our offer, I will give you a more thorough briefing en route and hopefully answer any questions you might have. At this point, suffice it to say that we feel we are on the verge of a very significant discovery." He paused to scan the faces around the table.

"I hope you won't think me given to hyperbole if I say perhaps we are on the verge of the most significant biblical discovery of all times. Jim, we need you to join with us. We want this quest to be documented photographically, and we need your skills in order for this to be a successful undertaking. Will you join with us?"

Jim tried to capture the right words. "Look, I'm sorry about the way I acted. I was wrong to have my feelings hurt . . . and yes, I will go with you . . . I *want* to go with you. And I'm fascinated by what you've said. But . . . I'm a little hesitant to ask. . . . Would it be possible to know *what* exactly we're looking for?"

There was no movement at the table for several seconds. Outside the window more than twenty floors below, the great city of New York was gearing up for another work day.

Dr. Crawford leaned forward. "Jim, perhaps you won't appreciate the significance of the possibility before us. It may seem trivial to you, I don't know, but again I will say, it is possibly the most important biblical discovery of all times. . . . We think we're on the verge of securing a manuscript of the Gospel of Luke—in Luke's own handwriting!"

# 2

Antas woke with a smile.

Even before he opened his eyes, he recognized the sound—a fitful humming only inches from his face. He leaned toward the small window by his mat and gently parted the curtain. There Antas saw what he had viewed each morning for the past few weeks—a single wasp going about her daily business of gathering material for building a nest.

Antas smiled widely when he saw the wasp, and whispering so as not to wake his wife and child, he spoke to the insect: "Ah, little bug with the stinging tail—even today you begin your work before me."

He watched closely as the insect attacked a single splinter on the rough-hewn lumber that framed the window. The wasp tugged at the wood fiber with its pincers, rolling her head side to side as her entire body rocked with the effort. The wasp was not actually trying to rip the fiber loose, but she was accumulating small bits of wood. Almost imperceptibly the powerful jaw muscles were extricating minute particles of the wood. Antas watched as the tiny mass of wood grew as the insect continued to struggle. When the accumulated mass was about the size of a small seed, the wasp abruptly flew off.

Antas knew the wasp was on its way to the nesting site to add one more small bit of pulverized wood to its construction. The nest was near the house, and Antas had often watched as the wasps constructed it. Thermion, who now lay sleeping at his side, had insisted he burn the nest, for she feared the insects' stings for the baby. But Antas had refused. The issue became a small joke between them—Thermion chiding her husband playfully, "You don't really love me—the wasps are still there," and then the two of them laughing.

Antas smiled again as he looked at his young wife sleeping at his side, her black hair framed her face. He thought of how those eyes, now closed, would sparkle when she teased him. Near her arm, in a tiny basket, was the baby, sleeping as quietly as his mother.

Quietly Antas laced his sandals, tied his cloak around his waist, and slipped outside.

The sun was only slightly above the small rolling hills—which could hardly be called hills at all—but Antas could feel the warmth on his face. Soon the little village would be warm

26

and alive with activity, but for the moment, Antas was the only witness to the Egyptian morning.

Not far from the acacia grove where his simple house was situated flowed a small stream, one of dozens that tapped the Nile before it emptied a dull stain of silt and mud into the metallic blue of the Mediterranean. Tracing a line through the arid landscape, the Nile River delivered a cargo of rainwater from the lush African interior. That water—the force of its flow dissipated as it fanned out near the great cities of Cairo and Alexandria—would seep into the alluvial marshlands and provide the nourishment for a very unusual plant that thrived in the sticky mire of the Nile marshes.

With its leafless, oddly triangular stem crowned with a delicate spray of foliage, the papyrus plant remained only an object of idle curiosity until a use for it was discovered. Cut into strips and pasted together with some sludge from the marsh, it was found that the plant could provide excellent writing material. This discovery had come to be of no small economic importance to the area, and an industry had grown up as the educated people all around the Mediterranean—kings and rulers with official court records, businessmen keeping accurate tallies, noblemen sending personal correspondence—all looked to Alexandria for their need of writing material.

Antas was one of those who helped meet that need, for he was a papyrus-maker and the son of a papyrus-maker. And on this early morning as he stood outside his rude hut, he was about to embark on a project that would have implications so broad that had he been

27

told, his simple heart would not have comprehended them.

"Today I will begin," he said to himself, "The time is right. I have waited long enough—I will begin."

He walked over to the wooden vat and slid the lid back to inspect the contents. There in the vat, immersed in the murky water, were several dozen papyrus stalks. Antas nodded in silent agreement with himself. "Yes, today I will make the finest papyrus ever made in Alexandria."

By the middle of the morning Antas had made great progress, for he worked quickly and efficiently. For more than two months he had allowed the reeds to soak, draining off the water as it became foul, and replacing it with fresh water. Prior to soaking the reeds he had taken much care to select choice papyrus. Then the outer layers had been peeled off to be used for other sheets of lesser quality—but the inner cores, closest to the pith, which were the most malleable and produced superlative writing materials—these Antas had placed in the special vat.

Finally after these long weeks of waiting and planning, Antas was now able to begin his work in earnest. Several times Thermion called him to eat his breakfast, but she eventually had to bring a dish out to him. "Who will take care of me after you've starved to death?" she teased.

Antas laughed heartily, kissed his wife, ate a few mouthfuls, and went back to work.

Thermion sat on a rock, observing her husband. She could not understand his preoccupation with this project. She had noticed how many times he had inspected the papyrus stalks during the past two months. *Perhaps a woman can't really understand a man's work,* she thought.

She watched as Antas took the oddly triangular strips of the papyrus—each about an inch wide and six to seven feet long—and placed them side by side. When he had constructed a sheet approximately a foot and a half wide, he began placing shorter strips at right angles to the first layer, carefully pressing the water-soaked papyrus into place with deft fingers.

"Now," he said to Thermion without looking away from his work, "I will show you how this will be better writing material than I have ever made." She watched as Antas first poured a bowlful of water on the sheet, and then began laying another layer of the long strips over that sheet.

"See, Thermion, this sheet will have three layers instead of two. It will be thicker and stronger than any I have made before, and when I have smoothed the surface, it should bring a good price when Demetrius takes it to the market."

At that moment the baby started crying and Thermion scurried back to their little house to provide his midmorning feeding.

Antas stepped back from the papyrus to survey his progress, and then began the laborious process of chinking the papyrus strips. He took small shavings of the papyrus plant, mashed them with a round stone, and placed them in the gaps between the strips.

Again and again he repeated the process: place the shavings in the cracks, soak the area with water, then mash the new material into the older until the soft, cellular fibers were enmeshed with each other.

He had often wondered if an entire sheet could be made by this method—and on a few occasions he had tried to pulverize the papyrus into a paste and then dry it, but he was not encouraged by the results. Still, it was a problem he thought of often, and he had determined that someday he would try again to develop this substance.

It was paper that Antas had in his mind. But although he understood the principle and would make a number of attempts later in his life to produce it, he would never develop a process of pulverizing a sufficient quantity of the papyrus stalks to make the effort feasible.

Antas would never know how close he was to the discovery of paper, but he could not have been happier if he *had* actually made the new substance himself. For although he would be a failure in the one project, nevertheless, he was, in fact, bringing the art of papyrus making to a new high.

Eagerly he continued to work, smoothing and polishing the finished areas with a mussel shell fashioned for the purpose. Occasionally he would splash water over the finished areas to keep them moist. He did not want the sheet to dry until it was laid out on the drying rack and pressed down flat.

For several days Antas continued his routine with the papyrus. Arising at first light, he labored with the strips: laying them in place, pasting, chinking, and polishing until the sheet met his high standards.

In the middle of the day, Thermion would

bring him some cheese and freshly baked bread and they would sit in the cool shade sharing their meal while the baby slept.

"Your work goes slowly," Thermion said, one day pointing to the papyrus.

"Do you think I am making fish wrapping?" he laughed. "No, it is going slowly because of the pains I am taking." Antas paused for a moment, took a bite of the bread, and with his eyes focused above the warm Egyptian landscape, he spoke again. "I cannot explain this, Thermion, but there is something special about this papyrus. I feel that God has given me special ability to make the papyrus and so I must make it."

"Tomorrow is the first day of the week. Will you abandon your papyrus long enough for worship?"

"Oh yes," he smiled. "Even God rested one day of the week."

The next morning Thermion awoke early to begin to prepare food for the fellowship meal. Several loaves of bread and some cheese would be her contribution to the community meal.

Later that afternoon they began their walk to Alexandria, a trek that would require only a little more than an hour. As they approached the city Antas noticed the pharos. A thin vapor of black smoke was the only signal from the four-hundred-foot-high lighthouse, but very soon Antas knew that the fire would be fueled and the blaze, reflecting off polished metal, would serve as a beacon visible to ships as far as twenty miles away.

As Antas entered the city gate, he felt a sense of pride to be a part of a city as splendid and as important as Alexandria. Not only was Alexandria the chief supplier for papyrus, but it was also known as the granary of the Mediterranean world.

He knew that if he walked farther down the street he would come to the great library known around the world. Antas himself could not read, but he felt a kinship with the intellectual center, and the men associated with it, for he, Antas, had some papyrus made by his own hand lining the massive shelves.

But his route this evening would not take him in that direction; instead he and Thermion turned right to head toward the house of Demetrius, near the harbor.

Demetrius had a large house, for he was a prosperous merchant. His effusive, outgoing spirit had served him well in his work, for he was one of only a few who had good relationships with both Greek and Jewish traders.

"My good friends Antas and Thermion!" Demetrius greeted them after a servant had led them through the foyer. Demetrius hugged Antas with his huge hairy arms and then they made their way through the courtyard to the dining hall.

Soon an assortment of nearly twenty people was assembled around a long flat table. A more diverse group of people could hardly be imagined. There were two young Roman soldiers; Ashtarak, the Phoenician ship captain, whose ship was undergoing repairs; Phila, the servant girl was there, as well as Ceranus and Elis, members of the ruling class; plus the two brothers Argos and Chios who were coppersmiths, with their wives; and also Mattaniah, the Jewish merchant, with his family.

Position and importance, wealth or the lack of it were to be transcended for a few hours as this unlikely amalgam of people shared their food and a few moments of worship together.

Demetrius, a giant, cheerful man, sat at the head of the table. His two sons served as attendants. When everyone was quiet he raised a loaf of bread over his head and offered the blessing: "Blessed be Thou, O Lord our God, and Father of our Lord Jesus Christ, who bringest forth bread from the earth." Then he turned to address the group of worshipers: "As we break this bread, may we remember that all the fragments belong to the loaf, and that we are all individual parts of the body of Christ." There was an assenting "Amen," and the bread was passed, to be followed by the dried fish, olives, oranges, dates, and cheese brought by various members of the group.

During the meal there was an informal sharing of news: the soldiers related the latest news from Rome—intrigues concerning Nero's court and news about the war in Armenia. The others shared news from their own particular spheres of interaction—news both grave and light, good and bad, with a particular emphasis on how the course of events affected the small group of believers and other groups like them.

Ashtarak, the sea captain, shared reports from several pockets of believers in port cities he had recently visited. "We should be thankful," he said. "In many places it is forbidden to worship as we do here. There are vicious rumors about our faith—some are saying that we offer human sacrifices. They misunderstand our baptism and spread rumors that we are drowning people. Likewise, because we talk of the blood of Christ, we are thought to be like some superstitious pagans who cut out the heart of a poor victim in an offering to their gods."

"It should remind us," Demetrius put in, "of how our Lord was misunderstood. Perhaps we cannot expect to be understood when the Son of God was crucified like a criminal."

"He was to be despised and rejected by men according to the prophet," Mattaniah said.

There was silent agreement by all those at the table.

When each one had eaten his fill, Demetrius stood and blessed the cup of wine in the same manner as the bread, and the cup was passed around the table as each one partook. Prayer was offered for each individual to live his life in such a way to bring glory to God and for other believers in other places, particularly those who were undergoing persecution. Finally the group joined in unison for their common confession: "He who was revealed in the flesh, was justified in the spirit, beheld by angels, proclaimed among the nations, believed on in the world, taken up in glory, even the Lord Jesus Christ, amen."

They stood and held hands around the table as they sang a hymn, and then the service of worship was ended.

"My friends," Demetrius said, "I have an announcement. I was given a message today, delivered by a seaman from a grain ship that docked only this morning. The message is from Apollos. Let me read it:

*Greetings to those of the household of faith, servants of the Lord Jesus Christ, citizens of Alexandria, who meet at the house of Demetrius. Grace to you and peace. I have entrusted this letter to the hand of a fellow Alexandrian, the captain of the ship, Pharillion. I hope to be aboard a sister ship bound for Alexandria in just a few days. With God's grace, I should arrive in Alexandria only a few days after you receive this letter. I look forward to sharing in your fellowship and your worship. Grace to you all.*

*Apollos*

There was considerable excitement among the small group of believers, for Apollos' reputation was well-known. A native Alexandrian of Greek ancestry and schooled in the classical Greek system, he had converted to Judaism while a student at the great library. Later he had embraced the message of Christianity wholeheartedly and become one of its most articulate spokesmen. Perhaps no one except Peter or Paul could have generated more excitement among the Alexandrian fellowship.

Soon individuals and families began filtering out of the house to their homes. Demetrius walked with Antas and Thermion into the cool Egyptian night. As the evening breeze brought the aroma of the Mediterranean Sea to their noses, Thermion secured the baby's wrapping as a protection from the night air. Across the harbor a great fire burned in the lighthouse.

"Antas," Demetrius said. "Will you be bringing some papyrus for me? I have a shipment of many items going north in a few weeks and I need some high-quality writing material, not the fish wrapping some try to sell."

"I am working on some very fine papyrus and I will have some ready when your ship sets sail."

"Very well, I will talk with you further in a week. The ship's departure date will be set by then. And don't forget—Apollos will be here to speak to us. Until then, may the Lord go with you."

"And with you as well, Demetrius."

Antas put his arm around his wife and they began their walk home. As always after these communion services, he felt as if a small flame in his heart had been stoked and fanned. He was both content and exuberant.

"Ah, Thermion, my wife, it is good to be alive."

Thermion smiled in the darkness, for she knew this was one of those effusive moments her quiet husband rarely demonstrated.

"God has been good to me," he continued. "I have you, and the baby, and I have my work. And of course these friends and the faith we share . . . and I have peace in my heart, except . . ." His voice trailed off into his thoughts.

"Except what, my husband?"

"Except . . . sometimes I feel I have too much. I sometimes desire to do something. I know I can't repay God—that is not possible—but I still would like to do something to make a contribution . . . to demonstrate my gratitude."

"According to what we are told," Thermion answered, "the Apostle Paul instructed believers to have faith in God, to live quiet and simple lives, and to be honest in all our dealings. You follow all these principles. Why would you seek to do more?"

"I don't know," he said. "But still . . ." and again his voice trailed off.

"We were also instructed," she reminded him, "to pray about anything that concerns us. Perhaps you should ask God what it is you should do, if you feel you must do something."

Antas stopped and put his hands on his wife's shoulders. "As always, my wife, you give me good advice. Now, let us hurry, or we will never get home."

The next week Antas continued to follow the routine he had established of rising with the sun to work on the choice papyrus, and working until he was no longer able to see the cracks. He did, however, devote some time to more conventional grades of papyrus, which he bundled and stacked for delivery to Demetrius. But his primary efforts were directed to *the* papyrus, and Antas labored over it, polishing the most minute rough spots, until the last available bit of daylight slipped below the Egyptian horizon.

On the first day of the week, Thermion arose earlier than usual to bake extra bread for the worship service. Later that day they made the familiar trek to the port area and Demetrius' house, where they were greeted enthusiastically.

"Ah, Antas and Thermion," Demetrius exclaimed, "how good to see you on this special day! Our guest, the eloquent Apollos is here; and Antas, after the service he would like to speak to you. He has something important to discuss."

"With me?" Antas stammered. He looked at his wife and then back at Demetrius. "Why would he want to speak with . . ."

"Never mind," Demetrius interrupted as he guided them into the house. "After the service. We'll talk then," and he turned to greet another family of worshipers.

Near the back of the dining area Antas and Thermion saw a small group of their fellow worshipers talking. In the middle of the circle was a young man perhaps thirty years of age who stood nearly a head taller than the others.

"That must be Apollos," Thermion whispered.

"Yes, it certainly must be," Antas answered. Antas understood with just one glance how Apollos had earned such a reputation in the athletic games. As the young man spoke, he gestured with massive arms and hands set upon a square, solid body. His thick cream-colored hair framed a face which betrayed his Greek heritage.

Antas had the distinct impression he had seen Apollos before, but as he thought about it more, he decided that Apollos bore a great resemblance to several of the Greek statues he had seen in the library courtyard, for certainly Apollos embodied the Greek ideal of athletic masculinity.

In a few moments Demetrius entered and began introducing Apollos to each of the worshipers.

"Ah, Brother Antas," Apollos said with a genuine smile and a vigorous handshake. "Demetrius has told me of you. I'm greatly pleased to meet you."

"And it's a great honor for us to have you here," Antas said, wondering why Demetrius would have told Apollos of him.

"I must speak to you after the service," Apollos said. "Perhaps you are the answer to our prayers," and just then Demetrius pulled him away to meet another family.

"What do you suppose he means?" Antas asked his wife.

"I do not know, my husband, but perhaps he will explain after the service."

In a few moments the communion service began and it followed the same quiet and gracious pattern as all previous services, except that at the end of the meal Apollos was given an opportunity to speak to the members of the fellowship.

"My dear brothers and sisters in Christ. Grace to you and peace," he began. "I am grateful to God for the opportunity to return to Alexandria, for as you may know, although God has seen fit to call me elsewhere, Alexandria is still my home. I spent several years here in the great library in a quest for knowledge. Since that time I have gained a true knowledge—the knowledge of God. For God, who created the universe and the people who inhabit it, has spoken to us in the past through the prophets, and has now spoken to us through His Son, Jesus Christ, who is the exact representation of the nature of God . . ."

In Antas' mind there could be no question of the sincerity of Apollos' words, for his blue eyes were aglow with enthusiasm for the message he was proclaiming. Apollos' address was not unusually long, nor was it complex—as might have been expected from one who had studied under the great Greek philosophers of the day, it was a simple message of God's grace poured out in the person of His Son to an undeserving people, with an emphasis on the resurrection being the affirmation of God's victory over death. Nevertheless, Antas had some difficulty concentrating because he was still wondering what Apollos meant when he said, "You may be the answer to our prayers."

After the service, Apollos spoke to Antas and Thermion as they were leaving. "Tomorrow I would like to come to your house, if it is possible. I have a matter of some importance I would like to discuss with you. Would that be possible?"

"Well, yes," Antas replied, still curious about what Apollos could have on his mind.

"Very well, then. Demetrius has consented to walk with me. We will see you in the morning."

The next day Antas rose early, as usual, although he had not slept well. His concern over Apollos' visit had robbed him of his usual rest. Nonetheless he laced his sandals and resumed his work with the papyrus.

Antas pulled back the sheets of inferior papyrus he used for covering his project. He stood for a moment examining his handiwork. The papyrus had reached its desired size. All that remained was some final polishing, then it would be ready for drying. "Two, maybe three days," he mumbled to himself.

The sun had not reached its zenith when Antas noticed two men making their way up the dusty road toward his house. He alerted Thermion, who was busily preparing a meal for the visitors.

Antas walked out to greet the two men and then led them to the shade of the acacia trees near the little house. Thermion brought them cool water from the cistern.

After the two men had quenched their thirst, Apollos spoke. "Brother Antas, Demetrius informs me you are a craftsman of the highest degree."

"I am afraid Demetrius has been in the business of buying and selling for too many years," Antas replied, "and perhaps he is given to exaggeration."

All three men laughed, Demetrius more than the other two.

"I tell you, Apollos—no matter what he says of me—Antas has the hands of the artist when it comes to papyrus. No one in Alexandria produces as high-quality papyrus as Antas."

"Let me come to the point," Apollos said. "I have need of high-quality papyrus such as Demetrius says you are capable of producing. You see, about two months ago I was able to spend a few days in Caesarea with our beloved brother, Luke, the physician. He has as his objective to record all the events of our Lord's earthly ministry. This is a worthwhile and much needed project, and no one is better suited to the task than Luke.

"During our time together he inquired concerning my itinerary for this journey. When I mentioned I would be in Alexandria, he immediately asked me to procure some writing material for him, since Alexandria is well-known for its papyrus. When I mentioned my need to Demetrius, he was quick to recommend. . . ."

"Please, come with me," Antas interrupted. He had been listening attentively, but could constrain himself no longer. Even as Apollos had been speaking, everything began to focus in his mind—here was the opportunity he had prayed for! *This* was to be the special purpose for the papyrus! What could be more important than recording the life of the Lord Jesus? His heart was pounding in joy and anticipation. All the uncertainty and confusion he had felt were swept away as the purpose for the papyrus crystallized in his mind.

"Look," he said, as he pulled back the covering over the papyrus. There were several moments of silence as the two inspected Antas' masterpiece.

"This is an extraordinary piece of work," Apollos finally said in genuine admiration.

"It is even better than I have seen you make before," Demetrius concurred. "And its thickness . . . is that not unusual?"

"I made it three layers for strength," Antas replied, still beaming not so much with pride as with sheer certainty.

The two men inspected how Antas had sandwiched one layer of short papyrus strips at right angles to the long strips.

"Antas," Apollos said, "while I was studying at the great library some years ago, I had the opportunity to read and study several thousand papyrus manuscripts, and I must say that none compared in quality or smoothness to this piece! You have exceeded the work of all the master papyrus-makers of

Alexandria. This would be papyrus *worthy* of the purpose Dr. Luke has for it—if you are willing to sell it. . . ."

"It is a gift."

"What?" Apollos said.

"It is a gift. I have prayed that God would give me an opportunity to express my thanks, and now He has given me that chance."

"But it would command an excellent price," Demetrius said. "Enough to provide for your family for many weeks."

"But no price could give me the joy I feel in my heart right now. I am only a simple man, my friends, but God has smiled on me, and the skill He has given me I now have the opportunity to give back to Him. Think of it! The words and deeds of the Son of God will be written on papyrus *I* produced, from the plants *I* cut and fashioned into this sheet! What price could ever give me such joy and satisfaction? No, it is a gift. It has no price."

The two men realized that there was no use arguing. "It is a great gift you are giving, my brother," Apollos said. "God will surely bless you for your generosity."

"I have already been blessed beyond my expectations," Antas replied. "But tell me, when do you need the papyrus?"

"I plan to sail one week from today—the morning after the worship service. Can you have it ready by then?"

"Oh yes, in two more days it will be ready for the final drying. Two more good days in the sun after that and it should be completely finished."

"Good. Then we will expect you and the papyrus for our time of worship next week.

God has truly answered our prayers!"

The next Lord's Day Antas sang the closing hymn of the worship service with additional vigor. After the service Demetrius provided a cedar box for the papyrus, and Antas presented it to Apollos.

Later he and Thermion walked home under a sky shimmering with thousands of stars. And as the heat of the earth dissipated into the cloudless sky, Antas the papyrus-maker, in his rude hut, slept a rare sleep—the sleep of one who was at peace with God.

# 3

Jim was seated on the aisle of the Boeing 747. At his side was Sarah, and Dr. Crawford had the window seat.

"I hope you will pardon me for requesting the window seat, Jim. It's a little fascination of mine—looking out airplane windows."

"My father," Sarah said, "often laughed about his and Uncle Enoch's first flight. They were both invited to some symposium and neither had ever flown. Uncle Enoch checked out all the books in the library on aerodynamics and related subjects, and then managed to get himself invited into the cockpit where he asked the pilot every imaginable question about flying! Father says Uncle Enoch is a philosopher in the true sense of the word— *philo-sophia*, 'lover of knowledge.' "

"Ah, say what you will," smiled the archaeologist, "but it's just the little kid in me. As a boy I would swing as high as possible in our backyard swing, but I could never swing high enough, nor stay up long enough to see all I wanted to see. This airplane affords me the opportunities to take those lengthy, detailed looks I could never get in that swing."

"Look," Jim said, "I have several dozen questions about this undertaking, but the first one is this: What's so doggone important about this manuscript? You were right when you said the importance of this mission might escape me."

Dr. Crawford leaned toward the younger man. "I suppose now would be the best time to give you a crash course, or perhaps that's not the most appropriate terminology," he chuckled, "considering we're twenty thousand feet in the air. In any event, you need to have a working knowledge in the area of manuscript research if you're to be effective. Before I try to answer your question about the importance of the manuscript, let me show you something."

The scholar fumbled through his briefcase and handed Jim two photographs.

"The first of these is a portion of the Gospel of Luke in the Codex Vaticanus, and the second is a portion of John's Gospel contained in the Codex Sinaiticus."

"What's a codex?" Jim asked.

"Simply a book," Sarah enjoined, ". . . as opposed to a scroll. The early Christian church popularized the codex form for their writings because it was simpler and less bulky than the scroll form which had been used for centuries."

"So how old are these manuscripts?"

"These two manuscripts both date around

46

A.D. 350 and are the earliest complete or nearly complete manuscripts we have," said Dr. Crawford.

"But you're saying the New Testament was written earlier than that?" asked Jim. "I thought I read somewhere that the New Testament wasn't written until hundreds of years after the fact, and couldn't be trusted. Is that true? Are you hoping to find this manuscript of yours in order to prove the Bible is true?"

Dr. Crawford laughed heartily. "No, I'm afraid the Almighty has not enlisted my assistance in determining His veracity. In one sense, I'm afraid it is impossible to 'prove' that the Bible—or any other book, for that matter—is true. The scientific method requires a repetition of the experiment, and history does not lend itself to being put in a test tube and subjected to a series of repetitions.

"The study I'm concerned with is much less ambitious. It is called textual criticism, which, very simply stated, is the effort to determine exactly what an author wrote. If we had the original autograph of every author's work—in this case the New Testament authors—there could be no dispute. But unfortunately for us, the ancient writers—both biblical and otherwise—did not have the printing press available and so copies of works had to be laboriously copied by hand—and human frailty being such as it is, mistakes crept in in some copies."

"Plus there's another kind of error," Sarah added. "Sometimes a scribe would maliciously change the text."

"Yes," said Dr. Crawford. "Unfortunately sometimes an unscrupulous scribe would vary the text or add portions to it in order to suit or give weight to his own particular theology. Some individuals felt perhaps that the Scriptures did not adequately enforce their own particular dogma, so they would bolster their case by adding to the record."

"Let me see if I understand this," said Jim. "What you're saying is that you have a certain number of manuscripts, some older than others, and very few, if any, say exactly the same thing; and what you're trying to determine is exactly what the original document said, even though hundreds of years have passed. It sounds like you've got your work cut out for you, Doc."

Dr. Crawford chuckled. "Perhaps it isn't as bad as you make it sound—although you have an idea of the problem."

"Let me use my uncle's illustration," Sarah said. "I've heard it often enough!

"Suppose, Jim, you are the teacher of a fifth grade class of thirty pupils, and in response to a letter sent by the class, the President of the United States sends a reply. That would be a pretty significant event. You decide to have the class copy the letter as a handwriting exercise, and everyone does so. The next day you discover that the janitor has inadvertently thrown the president's letter away. That, of course, would be a small tragedy, but the question is, Can you reconstruct the content of the original letter? Since you have thirty copies, it should be possible. So you instruct the class to hand in the copies made the day before. As you examine the copies, you notice that Johnny had failed to wash his hands after playing in the mud during recess, and therefore a portion of his copy is rendered illegible. Other papers have different but less serious problems: Mary neglected one entire line; others misspelled or omitted words.

"However," she continued, "because you have thirty copies, despite errors and discrepancies on several of them, it really is not a serious hardship to reconstruct the letter. While Mary omitted one line, twenty-nine others included it and the weight of the evidence suggests that that line was a part of the original."

"I see," Jim said. "But what about the New Testament? How many copies are there?"

"Jim," said Dr. Crawford, "there are over four thousand Greek manuscripts in whole or part."

"Four thousand! It doesn't sound like there'd be much of a problem reconstructing the original if you have four thousand copies to work with!"

"Perhaps not," said Dr. Crawford, "but there is one other element to be considered in determining the reliability of a work of antiquity—the amount of time elapsed between the original and our earliest extant manuscript. In the illustration of the school children, elapsed time was not a factor, since there was only a one-day gap between the original work and the copies. With ancient manuscripts, however, this is not the case."

"So," Jim said, "because so much time elapsed between the events in the Bible and the actual recording, you can't be sure that what is written is actually what happened."

"Actually, Jim," the professor responded, "that is not the case. Let me pick up Dr.

Bruce's argument at this point. He's one of the world's foremost authorities on Bible manuscripts. I often present his argument in my class." The professor took out a blank sheet of paper and wrote across the top:

| Work | Written | Earliest Copy | Time Span | No. of Copies |
|------|---------|---------------|-----------|---------------|

"Let's consider," the professor continued, "as Dr. Bruce has, a few works of antiquity. First of all, Caesar's *Gallic Wars* was written about 55 B.C. Our earliest copy dates around the middle of the ninth century and we have nine or ten good manuscripts. The *Histories* of Tacitus were composed around A.D. 100 and there are only two manuscripts, one from the ninth century and one from the eleventh. Likewise the *History* of Thucydides was written around 460 to 400 B.C. There are eight extant manuscripts of his work, the earliest from around A.D. 900.

"Now," the professor went on, "before we go on with the chart, let me show you a photostat of the earliest New Testament fragment we have." The professor reached into his case once again and pulled out a sheet of paper. On it were copied two scraps of ancient paper with Greek lettering.

"This is the John Rylands fragment," the professor explained, "so called because it is located in the John Rylands Library in Manchester, England. It is actually one fragment, not two—a portion of a codex leaf. It was written *recto* and *verso*—that is, on both sides. It is a small portion of the eighteenth chapter of John's Gospel."

"How old is it?" Jim asked.

"This fragment dates somewhere between A.D. 125 and 130. John is considered by most scholars to have been written no later than A.D. 85 to 90. So in this instance, we have a time span between the original composition and the first copy of not more than thirty-five to forty years."

When the professor had finished the chart, it looked like this:

| Work | Written | Earliest Copy | Time Span | No. of Copies |
|------|---------|---------------|-----------|---------------|
| Gallic Wars (Caesar) | 55 B.C. | A.D. 850 | 900 yrs. | 10 |
| Histories (Tacitus) | A.D. 100 | A.D. 900 | 800 yrs. | 2 |
| History (Thucydides) | 460–400 B.C. | A.D. 900 | 1,300 yrs. | 8 |
| Gospel of John | A.D. 85–90 | A.D. 125–130 | 35–40 yrs. | 4,000 |

"So you're saying that the Gospel of John stacks up better than these other works," Jim said.

"Not only the Gospel of John, but the entire New Testament. Compared to all other manuscripts of antiquity, the New Testament is by far the most well-attested work in terms of the number of extant manuscripts and the time span between the original writing date and the earliest copy we now have. These few works on the chart I chose as illustrations; I could have chosen dozens of others, but the comparison would have been essentially unaltered: the New Testament is in a category of its own in terms of manuscript authentification."

"That's pretty impressive," Jim responded, "but this is only a scrap!"

"Exactly," Dr. Crawford answered. "That's why we're enthused about the possibility of recovering the manuscript we spoke to you about." He leaned further forward and lowered his voice. "As I told you, we think it may be the original autograph of the Gospel of Luke!"

"I don't understand," Jim responded. "Where is this famous manuscript? Do you hope to dig it up? And what makes you think it's the real thing if you haven't even dug it up yet?"

"Actually, Jim, we are not going to 'dig it up,' as you put it. Here, let me show you something else."

The professor pulled two small black and white photographs from his case. The first showed an old Bedouin seated with a large scroll in his lap. Behind him was a young man, probably only a teenager, brandishing an ancient rifle.

"This photograph was probably intended only as a warning to us not to consider anything not on the up and up," the professor said, "but the second photograph shows the article for sale."

Jim studied the photograph closely. It was a close-up view of the scroll with its cover removed. The crusty paper revealed several rows of Greek letters.

"What does it say?" Jim asked.

"Let me interpret it for you, word for word," Sarah said. "I'll pick it up at the first complete line. As you can see, there are some illegible and missing words at the beginning. Transliterally, this is what it says: '. . . they from the beginning eyewitnesses and attendants having been of the word, it seemed good also to me, having been acquainted with all things accurately, with method to thee to write, most excellent Theophilus, that might know concerning which you instructed of things the certainty. There was in the days of Herod. . . .' That's the end of what is visible in the picture."

"Excuse my ignorance, but I take it this is from Luke's Gospel."

"Yes, it is," the professor responded. "The first complete line where Sarah began reading is part of the second verse in Luke in our Bibles. All of the first verse and some of the second have been destroyed by the centuries, but that is an incredibly small portion. We must expect that the rest of the text has remained intact, having been rolled up inside the outer layers."

"Yeah, but how do you know this isn't a fake? I mean, this crusty old desert rat might be trying to pull one over on the archaeologists."

"That was our first thought exactly, Jim," Dr. Crawford responded. "It has happened before, and none of us is invulnerable to being taken in by a hoax. But let me tell you why we think this is an actual first-century manuscript. One of the means that textual critics employ to determine the approximate dates of manuscripts is called *paleography*, which is

simply the process of determining a manuscript's age. A paleographer compares the letter size and form of the characters, plus other
things such as punctuation and text divisions,
with other writings of the period to determine
an approximate date.

"You see, Jim, Greek handwriting developed
through the centuries. In the second century
there developed a so-called 'biblical hand'
because of its widespread appearances in Bible
codices. However in the previous period the
Greek alphabet was more like an inscription—
more angular than the 'biblical hand.' Notice
the square *E*. It is much more representative
of the period of the first century or before,
than of the later period."

"You can tell all that from one lousy *E*?"

"No, not just from one letter—that wouldn't
be enough to be convincing. But the entire
passage that is visible lacks the flowing round-
ness of the later hand. Here, look at these two
samples of Greek handwriting." Professor
Crawford took out another piece of paper
from his briefcase.

"The first is a copy of the poem *Persae* by
Timotheus of Miletus, probably copied in the
last half of the fourth century B.C. Again, note
the thick blocklike strokes of that period. In
the right-hand column is the script from the
John Rylands manuscript you have already
seen. Notice again the change in the *E* and
also the employment of thick *and* thin lines in
the letter formations.

"It's our opinion," the professor continued,
"based on comparing these Greek characters
with other works, that this is indeed a mid- to
late-first-century composition. But that's not

"Fire away," the professor responded.

"First of all, why haven't you bought the scroll? I mean, why didn't you offer this old cameljockey four goats and a transitor radio? And if he wants central air-conditioning for his tent, give him that, too. Can't you meet his price? And the second question is, What in the world am I doing here? I hope you don't think I'm going to bargain for you. I'm almost as bad in that area as I am in reading Greek manuscripts. I've been cheated by hawksters on every continent on the globe."

"Let me try to answer both your questions," the professor interrupted, "because they are related to each other. In the first place, we haven't been able to meet the price because there is an unusual price. You see, our friend in the picture here, Ahmoud, wants his ancestral lands returned. According to him, his father was swindled out of his few paltry acres several years ago. The land is near our excavation site and it has changed hands several times since then, but Ahmoud says he will turn over the scroll when he has legal possession of the land. In effect, what we must do is buy the land and deed it over to him in exchange for the scroll.

"Which has turned out to be a more difficult proposition than we thought," the professor continued. "The present owner is an absentee landlord in Tel Aviv who is demanding a high price for the land, perhaps because he realizes he has something valuable there. We have the impression that he thinks we are American oil men and we have discovered oil on his property. We let him think whatever he wants, simply because we need to keep our actual mission in the utmost secrecy. But his belief that we're wealthy oil men skyrocketed the price. He wants over two hundred thousand American dollars for the property."

"Two hundred thousand dollars!" Jim exclaimed. "That's a lot of money for some crusty old papers."

"Actually, it's a real bargain," the professor responded.

"Yes," Sarah added. "The British paid the Russians a hundred thousand pounds—about half a million dollars—for the Codex Sinaiticus in 1947."

"Still, that seems like a lot of money," Jim added.

"It *is* a lot of money," the professor said, "as we found out when we tried to raise it the past few days—which is how you came into the picture.

"Because of the secrecy of the effort we couldn't afford to stir up interest in the press—you can imagine the confusion that would have resulted! Well, I was able to raise about half the sum needed through Sarah's father, a couple of trusted colleagues, and by taking some personal loans. Can you imagine my situation? Every additional person I contacted increased the possibility of the story leaking out. And every hour spent trying to procure the funds increased the possibility that something could go wrong with the manuscript. I became almost paranoid. I envisioned a fire destroying it or the old man suddenly dying, along with several other awful scenarios. What a tragedy it would be to lose the manuscript after more than 1,900 years!"

"But that still doesn't explain how *I* got into the picture."

"At this point," the professor continued, "my brother suggested your friend Alex and his magazine. He had served on a committee with Alex—I believe it was a fund-raising committee for the Special Olympics program—and had been impressed with the man. His reasoning was this: Rather than fear the press, we should make the press our ally. We made an appointment with Alex and offered him exclusive rights to the story in exchange for funding the additional hundred thousand dollars."

"I'll bet he snapped it up."

"Yes, I suppose you might say that. He plans to do a major story in the magazine and possibly a book later. And of course he is as anxious as we are to maintain confidentiality about the entire transaction."

"And my job, I suppose, is to document the goings-on with my camera."

"Precisely. And I might add we feel fortunate to have someone of your reputation along with us," the professor commented.

"Well, don't be too complimentary. Mostly I just point the camera and press the shutter release. The only difference between me and a lot of other photographers is that I've been stupid enough to go some places—at Alex's direction—that others were smart enough to avoid. And I'm beginning to realize I'm not getting any smarter. What an unbelievable assignment! I'm supposed to photograph a crusty old piece of paper in the possession of a crustier old sand rat who won't turn it loose until he gets his farm back. And all the while, we're to be nonchalant so as not to arouse suspicion! Alex has assigned me some doozies in the past, but this exceeds them all!"

"Just the same," the professor added, "your friend Alex has been very complimentary toward you and your skills."

"Yeah, and don't worry about Alex," Jim added, "he'll make some bucks out of this project, too."

"That will be fine," the professor went on. "I have no desire to make a profit from this venture other than the inestimable profit of being able to hold in my hands and to study this . . . this. . . ."

The professor had both hands in front of himself, cradling the imaginary scroll, but words failed him as he tried to describe it. He sank back in his seat. "Suffice to say, it would be a glorious and satisfying culmination to my life's work."

The professor removed his glasses and rubbed his eyes. "Young people, I think I should take a nap. I have not slept well the past few nights and we have much work ahead of us."

# 4

"Caesarea in sight!" The powerful voice of the seaman filled the morning air.

Apollos came onto deck just as the famous Caesarean theater came into view. He loved this city. To Apollos, Caesarea represented the best part of the Roman world. Certainly the Romans had been ruthless conquerors, but very often in the places of their conquest a sense of order and stability had arisen as the Roman soldiers kept the peace. And few places were better testimony of that order and stability than Caesarea—wide, clean streets; the hippodrome, site of the equestrian events; the theater and amphitheater, with rows of tiered seating for thousands; and one of the great marvels of Roman construction, the twin aqueducts—the great arched causeways that brought the precious rainwater from Mt. Carmel down to the city.

And, of course, the harbor. If the aqueduct

61

made life in Caesarea possible, the harbor made it profitable. The entire Mediterranean coastline from Egypt to Lebanon was like the blade of a great curved scimitar, practically bereft of any natural refuge for the sea traffic that moved along the coast. In Caesarea, Herod the Great had solved this problem by altering the coastline. Thousands of laborers had dumped tons of rock and debris into the sea to form a harbor, like a thumb and opposing finger, gently curled, and almost touching, that protruded nearly four hundred yards into the sea.

As the boat slipped through the narrow inlet into the protected waters, Apollos saw the most impressive Caesarean edifice of all—Herod's palace, which fronted the small bay. Its main chambers were now occupied by the procurator, Felix, and its dungeons contained a variety of prisoners, including a certain Paul—the most notorious member of a budding group called The Way.

As the boat docked, Apollos collected his belongings, including the papyrus made by the humble little Alexandrian, Antas. He was certain that Luke would be thrilled with it.

As he disembarked, he heard his name and looked up to see Aristarchus, the Macedonian, whom Paul had led to faith in Christ in Thessalonica, and who had been his constant companion and helper ever since.

The two men embraced heartily. Apollos, by far the larger, lifted his smaller friend off the ground and spun him around. "How good to see you again, my brother Aristarchus. And how is Luke? And Paul? And the rest of the brethren?"

"Fine, fine. They are all fine. But here, let me help you with your baggage. I'm glad you're back, Apollos. Luke was hopeful you would return this week."

"And how is Luke?" Apollos asked. "And how is he progressing with his work?"

"He has made several more trips to Galilee, and each time he returns he labors over his notes and records. Even this morning he is writing; but I think he is almost finished with his 'account,' as he calls it. He has instructed me to bring you to him as soon as you arrive. Did you bring him some papyrus?"

"Yes, some very fine papyrus."

Soon they had made their way through the streets to a small house not far from the interior of the city. There, in a cramped room on the second floor, the two men found Luke immersed in his work. He, with his back to the door, was oblivious to their arrival. Around him lay a number of written materials—vellum scrolls, a few papyrus works in codex form, and a great number of loose papyrus sheets. The ceiling was smudged with black and the room smelled of burnt oil, evidence of some late-night toil. The beloved doctor sat, reed pen in hand, intently transcribing some document. He paused for a moment, aware of a presence, and then turned toward the door.

"Apollos!" he exclaimed. "You're back!"

The two men embraced, and Aristarchus spoke. "Please excuse me. I know that you two educated men have much to talk about, and I will leave you to your conversation, for I need to go to the market to buy food for our brother Paul."

"You are a loyal and considerate servant of

the Lord, Aristarchus," Luke said. "When you return, we will take the provisions to him."

As Aristarchus left, Apollos said, "Tell me of Paul. How is he doing? And is there any hope of his release?"

"Come, sit down and I will tell you everything."

When the two men were seated, Luke spoke: "You ask of Paul and how he is doing. . . ." Luke stood again and walked to the small window overlooking Herod's harbor. Apollos looked closely at the doctor as he stood there, his lean, almost handsome face illumined by the midday sun. He seemed to be wrestling with a serious problem.

"Ah, Paul," the doctor said, looking out the window, "who can explain him?"

Apollos smiled. "Luke, I didn't ask you to *explain* Paul, I inquired as to his well-being."

Luke turned and smiled broadly as he realized Apollos' humor. "Of course you didn't ask me to explain Paul, and if you did, I would say he is unexplainable. Sometimes, Apollos, I think he is made of an altogether different material than the rest of us . . . but, yes, you asked about his well-being. His health is excellent and he is granted many privileges not afforded to other prisoners: he is allowed visitors daily and we are able to take him food. We will go there when Aristarchus returns from the market."

"Is there any hope Felix will release him?" Apollos asked.

"I don't know. At times I have sensed Felix would pardon Paul if he were offered a small bribe. Did you know he regularly summons Paul before him to hear Paul speak? I would *like* to think Felix is genuinely interested in Paul's message, but I think not. He seems to be concerned only with adding to his personal treasure, and *that* may prove to be his downfall. He is an inefficient administrator, and even now there are rumors that he will be recalled to Rome. So many complaints concerning his ineptitude have been brought against him by the military—surreptitiously, of course—that I wonder how much longer he can last. He has no real supporters.

"And I fear for Paul if Felix *is* indeed recalled, for he will have to come to some decision about what to do with Paul. He could release him, it's true; but he could also send him back to Jerusalem, and that would almost certainly mean death for Paul. Even now the Jewish religious leaders periodically send someone from Jerusalem to ask that Paul be returned for trial. Why they are so obsessed with him, I do not know. . . .

"But as for Paul, he seems impervious to it all. He has no fear for the future, and he seems to be perfectly content in his present state. I tell you, Apollos, a furnace burns within the heart of that man, and the flame is unaffected by any circumstances. Do you know what he told me? He said that in his weakness, he finds God's strength.

"But enough about Paul now. You will see him yourself when Aristarchus returns. He has asked about you often. Now, tell me of your trip to Alexandria. How is the church there?"

"First," Apollos answered, "I have something to show you." He reached into his baggage and pulled out the oilskin pouch. Inside

65

it there was a cloth covering, and when he unrolled it, there was the papyrus, coiled over a simple spindle. He handed it to Luke, and the doctor began to unroll it.

For a moment Luke was silent as he appraised the scroll; then he moved over to the window and let the midday sun shine on its polished surface.

"Such fine papyrus—I think I have never seen such quality," he said as his fingers tested the smooth edge of the sheet.

"Nor have I," Apollos responded. "It is the handiwork of a fellow believer in Alexandria."

"It is beautiful!"

At that moment they heard a noise on the steps.

"Ah, good," Luke said, "that would be Aristarchus. Let us go. I will show Paul the papyrus you have brought."

In just a few minutes the three men had made their way through the open streets and were standing before a small contingent of Roman soldiers. They halfheartedly inspected the basket of fruit and bread before admitting them to see Paul. A soldier led them down a cold, narrow stairway to the first level of the dungeon. Apollos kept his hands on the clammy rock wall as he allowed his eyes to adjust to the dim light. As they were led into a small alcove, Apollos caught a glimpse of Paul. He was only a few feet below them, but had not yet noticed their arrival. Seated on a bed of straw, he was taking advantage of some light filtering through a small air vent some twenty feet above his head. It would be a picture Apollos would carry in his mind for the rest of his life. Years later whenever Paul's name would be mentioned, Apollos would call to mind that brief glimpse of the apostle, his coarse cloak and a few scrolls set neatly beside him, devoutly pouring over the Scriptures in the poor light afforded him.

"The prisoner has visitors," the guard announced.

Apollos watched Paul carefully as he arose from the straw. There was a certain stiffness in his movements which Apollos attributed to the scourgings Paul had received. As a young boy Apollos had witnessed a scourging, and the poor victim had passed out on the twelfth blow, so the remaining blows were not accounted to him. It had been a revolting experience and had shocked Apollos' refined Greek sensibilities. He knew that Paul had endured this hideous torture on five different occasions and in each instance he had endured the full "forty less one" sentence. Apollos knew that these beatings must have left Paul's back a hideous mass of scar tissue.

Other than the rigidity he noted, Apollos thought Paul to be in excellent health for a man in his fifties. His pale arms, accented by thick wirelike hair, were as tight as a strong cord. Paul greeted first Luke, then Aristarchus, then Apollos: "Well, well, the giant Greek with the tongue of an angel. It is good to hear of your labor in the Lord."

Apollos had been an athlete and had wrestled opponents in many of the games, and he recognized the uncommon strength of the smaller man's grasp. And if there was strength in his wiry arms, there was raw power in his countenance. Luke was right—there was a furnace burning in the man—and the warmth of it was evident in his eyes.

"And tell me, my brother," Paul asked, "how are the brethren in Alexandria?"

"They do well. They are prospering under Demetrius' leadership and tutelage and are bearing a faithful witness to all who live in the area. They asked me to convey their love and prayers for you. They also asked me if there was any chance you would be released. It was a question I could not answer. How do you answer it?"

Paul paused for a moment. "I have not sought release. Why should I? I have all I need here. I am well provided for: I have food, the Scriptures, and I have a better physician than the emperor himself." He smiled at Luke. "My brother, Apollos," Paul looked at him squarely, "I have learned to be content in whatever my circumstances. I have been here nearly two years, but do not think God is unaware of my imprisonment or that He could not sever my chains if He so desired—but we must wait for His timing.

"No doubt it is best that I have been here, for Rome has protected me from my kinsmen—for as you know, I was as good as a dead man before Lysias brought me here. No, Apollos, I do not seek my release—I wait for His timing. But I think perhaps He still has an additional mission for me, and if I can be of any further service to our blessed Lord Jesus Christ, I would gladly go anywhere."

For nearly two weeks Apollos' life developed into idyllic predictability—the daily visits with Paul, visiting with members of the Christian community, and worshiping with them at the house of Philip and his daughters.

This peaceful string of uneventful days was broken by Aristarchus' shouts on the stairs one morning before Luke and Apollos had risen: "Luke, Apollos! Wake up, wake up—the Romans are here!" The two men got up quickly. Luke tried to calm the breathless Aristarchus.

"What do you mean 'the Romans are here'?"

"I went to the market early this morning. The news was all over the marketplace—Felix is being recalled to Rome! Porcius Festus has been named the new procurator of Judea. He arrived last night. Look for yourself." He pointed toward the window.

Luke and Apollos both stepped to the window to verify the report. There in the small bay was anchored a flotilla of Roman vessels, eight in all, four of them large warships with three banks of oars and a battering ram, and the other four, smaller attendant ships. All around the harbor were hundreds of Roman soldiers and seamen busily unloading the ships.

"What will this mean for Paul?" Aristarchus asked, his face betraying his fear.

"Felix has three choices, as I see it," Luke said as Apollos and Artistarchus turned to him. He spoke as if he had analyzed this situation beforehand. "He *could* release Paul, but I don't think that is a likely possibility—he would gain nothing from it. Or, he could send Paul back to Jerusalem—he knows as well as we, that would be certain death for Paul. But he dislikes the Jews and I doubt he would give the religious leaders that satisfaction. His third option is to leave Paul in prison with the matter unresolved, and I think that is what he will do. I think so, first of all, because Felix is probably preoccupied with saving his own neck right now, and secondly, because it would be an opportunity to leave a thorn in the side of his successor."

Both Apollos and Aristarchus nodded in agreement with Luke's analysis.

"However," Luke went on with a darkened face, "let us look at the situation Porcius Festus will inherit. He, in essence, will have the same three choices as Felix. And if he chooses to do the most politically expedient thing, he will turn Paul over to the Jewish authorities. They are the people who will have the greatest influence on the success or failure of his appointment, so why would he infuriate them by releasing Paul, or frustrate them by continuing to hold him in prison?"

"So you think it's inevitable that Paul will be turned over to the Jews?" Apollos asked.

"Put yourself in Festus' place. What other single act would better make the Jewish leaders look upon him with favor?"

"We must tell Paul," Aristarchus said.

"Yes," Luke agreed, "although he probably already knows."


"Do you think God has been caught unawares?" Paul was saying. "From the looks of your faces, I would say each of you had given in to despair. Do not think otherwise, my brothers, for my destiny is in God's hands alone. And do you think this turn of events has taken me by surprise? It was inevitable that Rome would recall the gluttonous Felix. Why should we waste our energy trying to determine what events await me? I tell you again, I am in God's hands, and I am sure. . . ." Apollos noticed Paul's eyes squint as he crystallized his thoughts. "I am sure He has something in mind for me. I cannot be sure what it is, but I somehow sense that I am on the brink of a major step in His plan for me. Now," he said with a tone of finality which evidently was meant to arrest any further concern for his welfare, "what have you brought me to eat?"

Apollos stood by the window watching the sun drop into the sea. As it dipped near the horizon it seemed to grow and intensify, and then as the fiery ball was dragged below the water line, the sky, for a few moments, was illuminated in purples and pinks. Then as those colors gave way to sicklier shades of yellow and metal-gray, a calmness pervaded the harbor town.

Apollos turned to Luke, who had lit two lamps, one on each corner of his work table. "Your work seems to be progressing."

"When I am able to concentrate, it goes well, Apollos. I only wish I had Paul's certitude about the future. I must confess, sometimes I fear the worst for him."

"You were certainly right about Felix," Apollos answered. "He was much too concerned about his own affairs to make a decision about Paul. I shall never forget watching him board the ship to Rome. I thought he would never be able to make it to the end of the pier! How many times did he stop to rest? Three, or was it four?"

A thin smile came across Luke's face at the recollection.

71

"Do you remember," Apollos laughed, "how he braced himself with those ponderous legs as he walked? And the picture of those seamen pushing him up the boarding plank—that scene would be the envy of every court comedian in the empire!"

They both smiled and then Apollos asked, "What do you know of our new procurator, Porcius Festus?"

"Very little, I'm afraid," Luke answered. "But I think we can determine one very important thing about him by his actions so far. Think about this, Apollos: How many days elapsed between his arrival and his trip to Jerusalem?"

"Three, as I recall."

"Exactly," Luke responded emphatically. "He hardly had time to unload his possessions and see that his troops were properly stationed, and then he was off to Jerusalem. And how long has he been there?"

"I suppose it's been a week," Apollos responded.

"A week and a day," Luke corrected. "And what does that tell us about the man?" Luke did not wait for Apollos to answer. "It tells us he is a much more calculating ruler than his predecessor—not that that is an attainment of any degree—but Festus recognizes the key to governing this area—pacifying the Sanhedrin! And what more soothing action could he take than to hand over Paul to their court? He doesn't even have to condemn him—simply send him to Jerusalem for trial. Of course the Jews are forbidden by Rome to carry out the death penalty—and since no other verdict would satisfy them, I would seriously doubt if

Paul would ever come to trial—his body would be found somewhere, the victim of one of the temple guard's knives."

There was a moment's silence as both men contemplated Paul's death.

"And what would be the cost to Festus? Practically nothing. He could wash his hands of the whole thing. 'After all', he could say, 'it is a religious question among the Jews—so they should decide the issue.' I'm afraid, my dear brother Apollos," he continued in a dejected tone, "Festus' lengthy visit in Jerusalem does not mean well for Paul." And he sat down at his table and continued the work on the manuscript.

At that moment Aristarchus burst into the room. "Luke, Apollos . . . Festus has returned! The Jews are with him. Paul has been summoned to appear tomorrow for trial!"

Apollos turned to Luke. "My brother, you have judged the procurator well."

The next morning Luke and Apollos made their way to the great marble palace and gained entry for the trial. The cavernous room was essentially empty except for a few guards. The two men unobtrusively took a position near one of the massive marble c_____ ___ in a few moments the courtly retinue began to arrive and place themselves around the white marble rostrum. Then came the members of the Sanhedrin, ten in all, with a few officials of the Caesarean synagogue, all grim-faced. Next came a small group of the Praetorian Guard in dress uniform, then finally Festus himself, attended by his advisers.

He was hardly seated when he made a perfunctory gesture to one of the court officials, who in turn motioned for the prisoner to be brought in. Paul, chained to a soldier, was led into the auditorium. As he stood at the foot of the rostrum, he did not look up at the procurator, but stood staring at his hands chained in front of him as though he were deep in thought.

The proceedings followed the traditional Roman pattern: first, the public *accusatio,* followed by the *interrogatio* of the judge, and the *excusatio* of the prisoner.

The Jewish leaders, however, had abandoned any systematic approach in their attempt to gain control of the accused, perhaps because they already had an agreement with Festus. Their accusations formed an invective rehashing of their previous charges: "He profaned the temple!" shouted one. "He serves another king!" said another. "He incites rebellion against Rome!" another added. "And he has broken our sacred laws!"

Apollos looked at Paul. He seemed to take no notice of his accusers or, for that matter, the entire proceedings. Apollos turned to Luke with the question on his face: What's the matter with Paul? But Apollos could see by the concern on Luke's face, that he could offer no reason for the odd behavior.

After several minutes of vehement railings at the chained man, Festus interrupted, as the echo of their accusations reverberated throughout the massive room.

"Prisoner," he said, "you may speak in your behalf."

There was a brief moment of hush in which Apollos fearfully believed that Paul was going to ignore the procurator. But Paul turned his face toward the dark-cloaked accusers and spoke deliberately and firmly: "I have committed no offense whatever; either against the law of the Jews or against the temple or against Caesar." Having spoken, Paul assumed his original posture.

Apollos noticed that Festus, obviously taken aback, shifted in his seat and leaned forward to address the prisoner: "As I understand the accusations against you, all of the charges brought against you are for purported actions taken by you while in Jerusalem. Now, I must ask you: Are you willing to go to Jerusalem and stand trial before me on these charges?"

Apollos saw Luke's hands lift in an uncontrollable gesture as the worst of his fears was about to be realized.

Paul spoke quickly, hardly before Festus had finished the query. If his voice had been flat and deliberate before, it was now vigorous and assured, infused with confidence and certainty. He gazed directly at the procurator as he spoke: "I am standing before Caesar's tribunal, where I ought to be tried. If I am a wrongdoer, and have committed anything worthy of death, I do not refuse to die; but if none of those things is true of which these men accuse me, no one can hand me over to them. I have done no wrong to the Jews, as you very well know. Therefore *I appeal to Caesar!*"

Paul's last statement triggered a reaction among all those present—the Jewish leaders huddled to try to understand exactly what Paul's statement meant; Festus, noticeably surprised at the prisoner's statement, called his counselors to him to discuss this sudden turn of events. Luke and Apollos looked at each other, and without speaking, realized what Paul had done: he had exercised his right as a Roman citizen to appeal his case to a higher court!

After only a few moments of deliberation, Festus turned to address the prisoner once again: "You have appealed to Caeser, to Caesar you shall go!"

The next afternoon Luke and Apollos made their daily visit to Paul, and when they returned, Aristarchus queried them as soon as they entered the door. "Did Paul say why he decided to appeal to Rome?"

Luke gestured in acquiescence to Apollos.

"He said he is convinced God wants him to preach the gospel in Rome. It is as simple as that," Apollos answered.

"What about the Jews?" Aristarchus asked.

"They left this morning," Luke responded. "We saw them at the palace. They were making another attempt to have Paul released to them. They were obviously upset that their plans had been thwarted. One of the procurators tried to explain that Paul, as a Roman citizen, has a legal right to appeal to Rome, but the Jewish leaders seemed to have little appreciation for the intricacies of Roman jurisprudence—they only knew Paul had escaped their malicious grasp once again, and they were seething in anger!"

"But when will Paul be sent to Rome?" Aristarchus asked.

"That's exactly the question we asked the procurator's legal counselor," Apollos said, "but he could give us no answer. He said they had received word that King Agrippa would be arriving in Caesarea in a few days, and the procurator would be preoccupied with preparations for that visit. He said the procurator will consider no other matters—including Paul's case—until after Agrippa's visit."

"I hope they don't wait too long," Luke said quietly.

"Excuse me, Luke," Apollos said. "What did you say?"

"The sea-lanes will be closed for the winter in a few weeks," Luke responded. "As you well know, the sea becomes a cauldron of storms from November through April. If a ship is to be sent to Rome in order to arrive before November, it should leave this week. Each day's delay makes it a more dangerous journey."

Apollos walked over to the window and peered out at the small bay and the great sea beyond. They were calm and serene now, but Apollos had traveled the sea-lanes often enough to know the truth of Luke's words— and for a moment, his mind conjured up an image of that great sea, foaming and th    h. in a violent storm.

5

They were met at the Tel Aviv airport by a tall black-haired man in his thirties. He was clad in faded khakis and gave Jim a vigorous handshake.

"Jim, meet Samuel Kavakis, my good friend and tireless coworker," Dr. Crawford said.

"Kavakis, did you say?" Jim asked.

"Yes." He smiled broadly displaying a mouthful of white teeth, contrasted against his dark features. "You will discover I have a rather checkered heritage. I am half-Jewish— that's my mother's side—and half-Greek, from my father's side. I am as thoroughly American as a Bostonian can be, but I am currently all Israeli and all Christian and the second best— excuse me, Sarah—the *third* best archaeologist in the country at this time. Specimens such as myself are rare, wouldn't you say?"

"Excuse me for interrupting this fascinating self-introduction, Kavakis," the professor said with a smile. "But I would be more interested in a report on the current status of the situation."

"Essentially the same," Kavakis said, turning serious. "The old man still will not allow anyone near his house. However his grandson—the one in the picture—walks over to the site almost every day to talk with us. He's a bright kid for a fourteen-year-old, and I think he's gaining confidence in us. We've assured him we're doing everything possible to get his grandfather's land back. I think he believes us, but his grandfather is getting impatient. So I think everything is still in order. . . . There was one incident day before yesterday, though, but I don't know if it's significant or not."

"Well, tell me, man," the professor said. "What was it?"

"Tuesday morning the boy showed up at the site and accused us of trying to steal the scroll. It seems his grandfather heard someone stirring around the house and he fired a warning shot with his old blunderbuss. I think we finally convinced the kid that we were not involved and hopefully he was able to reassure his grandfather. There is one thing that bothers me, though. One of our diggers mysteriously walked out on us that same night—which is not so unusual in itself, but it could be more than coincidence."

"So do you think the word has gotten around the site?" the professor asked.

"I think there are *rumors* going around. I doubt if anyone knows exactly what's going on, but it would be easy to realize something *is* going on—the almost daily meetings with

This area," he gestured out the car window, "has had the unfortunate circumstance of being a geographical conduit for three continents. Men and groups of men are funneled through here in the course of human activity. That, tragically, has resulted in almost continuous warfare for this land we now call Israel."

The car passed through acres of orange groves where young men and women were picking the large, luscious fruit. As the car moved further south, the terrain dropped off to a more arid landscape. Jim noticed acres of well-tended grapes and olives forming a pattern like a rumpled quilt.

Soon Jim began removing his coat.

"Jim," Kavakis said, "you won't be needing that coat again for a while. You'll find the temperature much warmer in this area. We're getting close to the lowest surface point of the planet—the Dead Sea, 1,290 feet below sea level."

Before long they came to a sign:

WELCOME TO JERICHO,
WORLD'S OLDEST CITY.

"So how old *is* Jericho?" Jim asked.

"About eight or nine thousand years," Sarah answered.

"But the claim is a little misleading," Kavakis added.

"Yes," the professor said. "There are actually three Jerichos—Old Testament Jericho, New Testament Jericho, and present-day Jericho—but they're all in general proximity, so I don't think 'oldest city' is an extravagant claim."

From Jericho the car headed due south through parched hills until the Dead Sea came into sight. It was flat, lifeless, and surrounded on both sides by dry, desiccated, lunar landscape.

"Welcome to Qumran," Kavakis said.

"Qumran?" Jim said. "Where have I heard that name before?"

"This is the site where the so-called 'Dead Sea Scrolls' were found," Sarah answered.

"Oh yes, everyone's heard of the Dead Sea Scrolls," Jim said. "But I couldn't for the life of me tell you why they're significant."

"The story of the discovery of scrolls," the professor said, "is an incredible story. It has all the elements of a great work of fiction— war, intrigue, subterfuge, and everything else—but the story is true."

"Didn't a little boy find the scrolls?" Jim asked.

"The actual facts," the professor went on, "have been difficult to authenticate, but the account that has been generally accepted concerns a Bedouin boy with the unusual name of Muhammed al Dbin, or Muhammed the Wolf. His family belonged to a group of contrabanders, who, in the spring of 1947, were smuggling goats and other goods out of Transjordan into Palestine. They had floated their commodities across the Jordan and had come to Ain Feshka—very near here—to fill their water bags before going on to B_____ to sell their goods on the black market. Muhammed had been assigned to mind some of the goats. Climbing up after a stray, he came upon a small cave and dropped a rock into it.

thousand pounds for just *one* of the Dead Sea Scrolls."

"What's so important about the Dead Sea Scrolls?" Jim asked.

"Before I answer that question, let me continue my explanation of how the scrolls came to light. Please understand that the version I have given you is one of three or four that differ in particulars, but not in substance. During the next few months it was impossible to move about the country—the turbulent political situation had erupted into a full-scale war. In early 1949, Ovid Sellers, from the American School, and his wife set into motion their plans to visit and excavate the site. A Bedouin guide offered to take them to the site but he demanded a high payment—including a portion of the finds. It was several months before something could be worked out and the area was secured and excavation was begun."

"They found some very interesting artifacts when they got into the cave," Kavakis said.

"Oh, what was that?" Jim asked.

"Well, among other things," Kavakis said, "they found some food-stained newspapers and a cigarette roller."

"Oh no," Jim said.

"Oh no is right," the professor said. "The entrance to the cave had been enlarged to make it easier to get in. . . ."

"And to get things out," Kavakis added.

"Were some of the manuscripts taken?" Jim asked.

"A number of them were spirited out," the professor replied. "Some were later recovered, but we have no way of being sure that all of them were. One scroll, the Temple Scroll, was purchased from the Bedouins in 1967. It conceivably could have been removed from one of the caves during the early months after the original discovery. Who knows? There may be others that have not yet come to light."

"You said *one* of the caves. You mean there's more than one?" Jim asked.

"Yes, there is more than one," the professor answered. "In fact the area is a virtual honeycomb of caves. There are more than two hundred in the immediate area, and each of those were to yield numerous documents—both biblical and nonbiblical."

"I don't think you've answered my first question yet," Jim said, "about the significance of the scrolls. But I've thought of another one: *Who* put the scrolls in the caves?"

The professor laughed. "More than one of my students has accused me of giving the necessary background for answering a question, but failing to answer it because the bell rung. Since no bell is going to interrupt *this* discussion, I assure you I will answer your questions. But let's walk up to the excavation site as we're talking."

The group of four made their way up the dry slope. "Jim," the professor said, "the discovery of the Dead Sea Scrolls is without precedence in the history of archaeology. Few would argue that it is one of the greatest archaeological events of the century. As an example, consider the Isaiah Scroll. Up until its discovery our oldest Isaiah dated about A.D. 900; the Isaiah Scroll has a probable date of around 125 B.C.—that means the date of our oldest extant manuscript was pushed back a thousand years! I could tell you of other similarly remarkable results from the find, but I want to be sure I answer your second question, 'Who put the scrolls in the cave?'

"Look at our excavation site," he continued. They had reached a small plateau and there were about a dozen young people, obviously American, who were some of Dr. Crawford's students, working at the site. There were a series of short walls of varying geometric shapes—squares, rectangles, and even circles— none more than waist high, the ruins of a small community.

"This was the home of the Essenes," Dr. Crawford said.

"Of whom?" Jim asked.

"The Essenes—a sort of back-to-nature commune of the first century before Christ. In several ways they were not too dissimilar to some modern religious communes. They considered society to be defiling, so they withdrew from everyday life to have a culture of their own. Their life was characterized by disregard for materialism, a fervent piety, devotion to the community, and an expectation of a coming messiah."

"What happened to them?" Jim asked.

"When the Romans decided they had had enough of Jewish obstinance," the professor went on, "they came through this area, and the Essenes, although they were bitterly opposed to the Jewish leaders in Jerusalem, probably realized that the approaching Tenth Roman Legion would not make that distinction. So, in the year A.D. 68, they evacuated this little spiritual outpost. No doubt their plan was to reassemble after the clouds of war had passed—that is why they hid their sacred scrolls in the caves—so they could return to their monastic way of life when the time was right. But that time never came, and they never returned."

There was a break in the conversation as the four stood looking at what remained of the small community that had thrived there in seclusion for more than a hundred fifty years—foundations of small houses, a larger foundation for the community center, the circular bases of cisterns, and the rock-carved ditches that provided the water for the community—all laid out in a neat, functional manner.

"It's tragic, isn't it?" Jim said.

"Yes, it is," the professsor agreed. "I don't want to glorify the Essenes—they were extremely legalistic and maybe a little mean-spirited as we've learned as we've read their writing, but it is indeed tragic that a group of people who had absolutely no interest in the political world found themselves trapped between two factions of the world they had renounced.

"Our excavation is not an ambitious project," the professor went on. "These are undergraduate students for the most part, doing necessary field work for their degree. We are working very deliberately and very meticulously, not so much for what we might find, but to teach the next generation of archaeologists the skills they will need. So we are more of a laboratory than a serious archaeological dig. The site was excavated in 1949 by Harding and deVaux, in 1951 by the École Biblique, and several times subsequently. We do not have great expectations for discovery, but it is a tremendous educational experience for the students."

"I hate to interrupt," Sarah said, "but we need to get organized. Tomorrow will be a full day."

"You are right, Sarah," the professor said. "There will be much to do tomorrow."

As they walked down the slope, Dr. Crawford spoke: "It's curious, Jim. I was explaining to you about our limited expectations, and now we are on the verge of possibly the greatest manuscript find since the scrolls were discovered in these caves! I'm sure," he said as he smiled and slapped Jim on the back, "there is a great spiritual lesson here somewhere—something about expectations and realizations—but I'm afraid I don't know what it is."

The next morning Jim was awakened by Samuel Kavakis. He looked at his watch. It was still set on New York time. He tried to figure the difference in time zones, but his fuzzy head wouldn't cooperate.

"It's a little past seven o'clock," Kavakis said. "Extremely late at an archaeological site. We usually begin the day at five, but the professor thought a couple of extra hours of sleep might help you fight jet lag. He and Sarah will be in the kitchen in a few minutes if you'd like to join us."

Jim dragged into the dining area, eyes puffy and face unshaven. He saw Dr. Crawford sitting in the corner with a book in front of him. Jim poured a cup of coffee and walked over near the professor. He saw that the book was a Bible.

"I hope I'm not disturbing you, Professor."

"Oh, Jim, good morning. Please have a seat. I was trying to recharge my spiritual batteries, as one of my students puts it."

"I think there must be more to what you're doing than just academic interest, Professor."

"Do you mean my Bible reading?" he asked with a smile. "I have cultivated this habit through the years. Let me read what David said about the morning: 'In the morning, O Lord, Thou wilt hear my voice; In the morning I will order my prayer to Thee and eagerly watch.'

"I have tried to follow David's example," the professor added, "and I get special pleasure from reading the Scriptures when I am here . . . in this land. What a magnificent place! It's hard to take a step in this country without crossing the path of someone whose steps are recorded here in these pages," Dr. Crawford said as he pointed to his open Bible, the pages dog-eared from much use.

Kavakis took an orange from the bowl. The sweet astringent vapor of the fruit filled the air as he peeled it. "Yosuf, Ahmoud's grandson, came into camp early this morning. He says his grandfather will let us look at the scroll tomorrow."

"That's great news!" the professor exclaimed.

"Yes, it is," Kavakis agreed. "I'm leaving now for Tel Aviv. I want to make sure all the legal work is in order."

"Do I need to go with you?" the professor asked.

"No, I don't think that will be necessary. You might as well stay here. I don't think there's anything to do now except wait."

"I almost forgot," Jim said, "but I'm on an assignment here, and I'm sure Alex would appreciate if I brought back a few pictures."

"Of course." The professor smiled. "I'm sure you need some background photos. May I suggest some shots of the work going on up the hill; and then perhaps Sarah would be willing to drive you around the area."

"Certainly," Sarah agreed. "We'll drive down along the sea and take the cable car up to Masada. That would be the ideal place for landscape shots."

Two hours later Jim was seated in an open Jeep streaming down the two-lane highway with Sarah at the wheel, her sun-streaked hair blowing in the wind. In less than an hour they came to Masada and boarded a cable car for the ride to the top.

The top of the hill was flat as a board and afforded a panoramic view of the area. The Dead Sea, a murky blue, was surrounded by stratified hills of varying hues of orange and pink.

"Herod built a fortress here," Sarah said. "That's what you see excavated."

Jim surveyed the low walls of several buildings over the flat mountaintop.

"Herod must have been somewhat paranoid," she went on. "He built this as a refuge for himself in the event of a revolt. It had been a modest fortress of the Hasmonaean Jews prior to Herod, but when he saw it, he recognized it as a strategic fortress, strengthened its fortifications, expanded the cisterns and storage bins, and turned it into a small city. He even had a Roman bath built. Over

93

there," she said pointing, "you can see the ruins.

"When the Jews revolted, the Zealot Menahem ben Judah led a group that stormed and conquered Masada. He distributed the weapons they captured and then led them to Jerusalem. When the Roman legions came pouring out of Caesarea, however, the Zealots had to retreat. Masada became their final stronghold. After quelling the revolt else-where, the Romans then turned their attention to Masada.

"If you look there," she continued, "you can still see the outline of the trenches the Romans dug around their base camp."

Jim looked at the square, still visible after two thousand years. "What happened then?"

"The Zealots were led by Eleazar ben Yair," she answered, "who was determined to de-fend Masada. And they were able to defend it for many months, but the Romans below were in no hurry. After a few unsuccessful attempts to scale the cliffs, they settled in to build an earth ramp to the top, using, for the most part, captured Jews as slave labor. After months and months of patient labor, the ramp was complete and the Romans rolled their war machines up the ramp. Surprisingly, there was no resistance. When the Romans poured over the walls, they were not at all prepared for what they found."

"What was that?" Jim asked.

"Mass suicide," Sarah answered. "Rather than submit to Roman slavery, the Jews at Masada killed themselves. The children and women were put to the sword first; then the men, after razing the mountaintop, put each other to death. The Zealots left ample supplies of food and water to demonstrate their defiance of Rome—that they had died willingly, rather than submit to slavery."

Jim felt a gnawing sickness crawling around inside him as he pictured the scene the Romans discovered. He had experienced it before—in Vietnam, South Africa, El Salvador, and elsewhere. He considered it the ultimate absurdity—human beings killing other human beings.

At that moment Jim was shaken out of his thoughts by the earsplitting scream of two Israeli F-4's that rolled only a hundred feet over his head.

"What in the. . . ?"

"It's a salute," Sarah answered when the noise subsided. "This is almost holy ground to the modern Jewish state. Every Israeli officer has his swearing-in ceremony here atop Masada. The byword of the Israeli armed forces is 'Masada will not fall again!' Every jet passing in this area does the same thing—a complete roll in honor of those who died at Masada."

Sarah led Jim around the plateau as he took shots of the various battlements and foundations, and jotted down notes as she explained.

"Here," Sarah said, "is the main cistern. It was carved out of solid rock. Supposedly there was a two-year supply of water for Herod and his complement of nine hundred men, if it was needed."

"May I ask you something?" Jim said, turning to Sarah.

"Sure."

"Why do you do this?"

"Do what?" she replied.

"Dig in the ground for old scrolls and old coins and . . . and whatever else old things you find."

Sarah laughed. "It *is* a rather absurd preoccupation, I suppose. My uncle's answer to that question is 'compulsive curiosity.' "

"Speaking of your uncle . . ." Jim said, "and I want you to know I like him very much. . . ."

"Most people do," Sarah said.

"But why would he spend *his* life digging up all these ancient things, too."

Sarah paused for a moment before she spoke. "As for me, I have known little else. I practically grew up on archaeological sites. My father does very little excavating now—he teaches and lectures primarily—but when I was a child, we spent every summer, and on two occasions, the entire year here in Israel or Turkey or Egypt. So it was only natural, I suppose, for me to follow in the archaeological footsteps of my father and uncle.

"As for my uncle," she continued, "I would not pretend to speak for him, although I have heard him answer the same question dozens of times. Perhaps you can ask him yourself tonight."

"I suppose it has to do with the nature of Christianity," the professor was saying. He, Jim, Sarah, and Samuel Kavakis were lingering over their tea after the evening meal.

"Explain, please," Jim said.

"Christianity is a *historical* religion," the professor said. "It is not simply a condensation of moral platitudes, or just a system of ethics.

Certainly morality and ethics are a portion of Christianity, but the core of Christianity is this: God has revealed Himself. He has revealed Himself in time and space and history. He has *intervened* in history, we might say.

"God could have chosen to give us His revelation in the form of a theological textbook, but he didn't; instead He set his revelation in history—He intervened in the course of events of human activity. The greatest culmination of that intervention, of course, is in the person of Jesus of Nazareth. My life's work has been to grub about in the skin of the earth, to find in that repository the bits and pieces relating to His life."

There was a moment of silence around the table, then Jim asked, "Tell me, professor, if you recover this scroll, do you think the Bible will have to be updated?"

"You mean do I think I will find something in the manuscript that differs from the Gospel of Luke as we know it? No, I don't think so."

"But you mentioned earlier the possibilities of changes being made—both intentionally and unintentionally."

"Yes, I did," the professor answered. "But I don't want you to think the problem is worse than it is. Let me explain. I have sometimes startled my textual criticism class by announcing at the first session that it has been estimated that there are a hundred fifty thousand variant readings of the New Testament. That catches their attention, I assure you."

"But are there really a hundred fifty thousand variations?" Jim asked.

"Let me explain it this way: Suppose a scribe in the eighth century, for example, misspelled a single word when transcribing the New Testament. Suppose then, that copy was used as the model for four thousand subsequent copies—that would count as four thousand variations.

"In actuality, the New Testament has incredibly few disputed readings—almost all of the variations have to do with spelling or word order. Schaff, the New Testament Greek scholar, says that only fifty of the variations are of significance, and none of these alter any precept of the New Testament. On the final day of my textual criticism class, I like to quote Sir Frederic Kenyon, the great textual critic. 'No fundamental doctrine of the Christian faith rests on a disputed reading. It cannot be too strongly asserted that in substance, the text of the Bible is certain.'"

"The Jews were very exacting about how the Scriptures were copied," Kavakis interjected, "and for the most part, their carefulness was imitated by the Christians."

"There was an intricate system," Dr. Crawford added, "that a Jewish scribe adhered to when he transcribed the Scriptures. He was required to wash his entire body and then don full Jewish dress. His parchment had to be prepared from the skin of a ceremonially clean animal, tied together by strings made from skins of clean animals—and this work had to be done by a ceremonially clean Jew. He was required to use only black ink of a specific recipe. He was not to write a single letter, not even a yod—the tenth letter of the Hebrew alphabet, which looks similar to our apostrophe—without looking at the text before him."

"Sounds like a pretty boring desk job," Jim said.

"I'm sure it was," the professor laughed, "which may have been the reason the Masoretes developed their systems of checks for the text."

"You lost me, Prof."

"You can't be associated with biblical texts very long without hearing 'Masoretic text.' The term is from *massora* which simply means 'tradition.' The Hebrew Bible was referred to as the Masorah.

"The Masoretes were a group of Jewish scholars concerned that the text of the Scriptures be preserved, so they took upon themselves the responsibility for that preservation. They were well-disciplined and they developed an unusual system of checks to determine that a new copy of the text was identical to the model. As someone said, everything that could be counted, was counted. They counted the number of times each letter of the alphabet appeared in each book. They numbered the verses, words, and letters of each book. The middle word and letter of each book was calculated. Dozens of other calculations were made, which we may justifiably consider trivial—but it had the desired effect: it preserved the text."

There was a moment of silence before Jim spoke: "Speaking of texts, I think I should read Luke's Gospel—as background for this assignment."

"Excellent idea, Jim. I have a New Testament you can borrow. Why don't you come with me to my room."

The professor took a modern-translation New Testament from his bookshelf and gave it to Jim. "I think you will find Luke to be fascinating reading—he is an unusual author."

"Why do you say that?" Jim questioned.

"First of all, because he was an unusual person. He was the only writer of the Gospels who had received a classical education—and his writing demonstrates his background. Someone has said, 'The richness of a man's vocabulary is a fair measure of his culture,' and that is proven in Luke's writing. The Gospel writers each use individual words peculiar to his Gospel—Mark forty-five, John about fifty, Matthew nearly seventy; but Luke utilizes nearly three hundred words peculiar to his Gospel. Also, tradition credits Luke with writing hymns and with painting. Rossetti's poem says:

*Give honor unto Luke, evangelist,*
*For he it was, the ancient legends say,*
*Who first taught Art to fold her hands and pray.*

"Another characteristic of Luke's record is his attention to detail. You will find repeated instances in which he will fix an event by tying it to a place, a person, or another event—a practice which, oddly enough, served to discredit him in theological circles in the past century."

"Why so?" Jim asked.

"Well," the professor began as he leaned back in his chair and motioned for Jim to have a seat, "the Tübingen theologians—Tübingen is a German University—were of the persuasion that Luke's two works were second century compositions. Their basis for this conviction was their inability to verify a number of the specific political and cultural allusions in his record. For example, in the seventeenth chapter of Acts, Luke refers to the *politarch* of Thessalonica. It was a term unknown in classical literature and considered to be an anachronism. Subsequent archaeological studies, however, have found nearly two dozen references to a *politarch* during this period. Interestingly enough, five of these references concern Thessalonica.

"Another example would be Luke's reference to Lysanias, 'the Tetrarch of Abilene.' The only Lysanias known to historians died in 36 B.C. The Tübingen school considered this another example of a second-century author muddling the facts. However, in 1929 a group of archaeologists digging near Damascus found an inscription dating about A.D. 20 referring to 'Lysanias the Tetrarch,' and Luke was vindicated again.

"Another time Luke was thought to have flunked geography. In Acts he refers to Lystra and Derbe as being *in* the district of Lycaonia, but the city of Iconium lying *outside* that district. That contradicted Cicero and other Romans who said Iconium was in Lycaonia. However, Sir William Ramsey in 1910 discovered proof that Iconium was indeed a Phrygian city during Paul and Luke's visit. Other archaeologists have subsequently verified this same fact.

"Speaking of Ramsey . . . ," the professor said as he jumped up and fingered through the volumes on his bookshelf. "Ah, here it is," he said taking down a book. "Sir William

Ramsey was one of the great archaeologists of all times. If we ever have an archaeologists' Hall of Fame," he said, smiling, "as we do for baseball and football, then Ramsey will be one of the first inductees. It is a rather fascinating story how he joined the Luke 'fan club.'

"Ramsey was trained in the German historical school and as a result was taught that Luke's Gospel and the Acts were mid-second-century compositions. However, he soon changed his mind. Here," he said, giving Jim the book, "read this portion."

Jim began reading aloud at the paragraph Dr. Crawford designated.

*I may fairly claim to have entered on this investigation without prejudice in favour of the conclusion which I shall now seek to justify to the reader. On the contrary, I began with a mind unfavorable to it, for the ingenuity and apparent completeness of the Tübingen theory had at one time quite convinced me. It did not then lie in my line of life to investigate the subject minutely; but more recently I found myself brought into contact with the Book of Acts as an authority for the topography, antiquities, and society of Asia Minor. It was gradually borne upon me that in various details the narrative showed marvelous truth. In fact, beginning with a fixed idea that the work was essentially a second-century composition, and never relying on its evidence as trustworthy for first-century conditions, I gradually came to find it a useful ally in some obscure and difficult investigations.*

"To publish that," the professor said, "required great intellectual courage, for it ran contralaterally to everything he had been taught, and it put those who had instructed him in very awkward light. But there's more—read this."

*Luke is a historian of the first rank. Not merely are his statements of fact trustworthy; he is possessed of the true historic sense; he fixes his mind on the idea and plan that rules in the evolution of history, and proportions the scale of his treatment to the importance of each incident. He seizes the important and critical events and shows their true nature at greater length, while he touches lightly or omits entirely much that was valueless for his purpose. In short, this author should be placed along with the very greatest of historians.*[1]

"Luke was an observant man," Dr. Crawford said, "a meticulous man, and a good man. He had that rare mix of artist and scientist. As someone once said, 'He loved the good, the beautiful, and true.' Beyond that, he was a gifted writer: *'C'est le plus beau livre qu'il y ait.'* "

"Pardon me, Doc. My French isn't what it should be."

"I'm quoting Joseph Ernest Renan. Of Luke's Gospel he said: 'The most beautiful book ever written.' "

[1]William H. Ramsey, *Saint Paul the Traveller and the Roman Citizen* (Grand Rapids, MI: Baker Book House, 1962), p. 7. (Cited by E. M. Blaiklock, *Layman's Answer* [Valley Forge, PA: Judson Press, 1970]).

6

To most excellent Terentius, member of the Senate
of Rome, legatus of the Augustan Cohort, and
brother of my father.

From Julius, centurion of the Augustan Cohort,
in service of the Emperor Nero in Caesarea of
Judea. Herod Agrippa and Porcius Festus send
their greetings, as do all those fortunate to serve in
the Augustan Cohort.

Sent by the hand of my trusted servant, Marcus.

Dearest Uncle, perhaps an apology is in order for
the late date of the completion of my most recent
duty, but I shall not offer it, for my service to
Rome has been honorable and exemplary, and I am
fortunate to have occasion to report to you at
all . . . fortunate that my rotting carcass did not
drift to some desolate shore to serve as a sour meal
for the shellfish.

Yes, noble Uncle, I despaired of my life and the
life of those entrusted to me, and my intention is to
chronicle the events that led to that point of

105

despair, as well as the subsequent events of our journey. I know you have received a cursory report concerning those events, but I will give you a more detailed account of our journey, and, if I may, I will venture some observations and opinions concerning the political situation in Judea. As you know, my service in the land of the Jews was not lengthy, nor am I an expert on administrative affairs, but since you have asked me to be your eyes and ears in this outpost, I will take the commission seriously.

When I arrived in Caesarea, there were two immediate surprises: the beauty of the city and, in contrast, the deplorable condition of the government. From the senate's perspective, it may have seemed wise to appoint a Roman who was married to a Jewess to administer that area, but Felix was the wrong Roman, and Drusilla, simply because she was married to a non-Jew, was the wrong Jewess. You see, those Jews who have any authority (and cause all the trouble, I might add) are the religious leaders; and according to them, their law expressly forbids them to marry out of their race. So you can see, Rome's attempt to identify with the Jews through Drusilla was destined for disaster. She is an outcast, and doubly so, for she had been married previously and divorced, which again, is forbidden by their law.

And as for Felix, or Antonus Claudius, as he was known in Rome, I can truthfully say he had endeared himself to no one, and expanded nothing except his already prodigious girth. I am sure Rome will be much better represented, and Judea much better governed, under Porcius Festus.

But I spoke of the city, noble Terentius, and Caesarea is a beaming jewel. I hardly believed such a remote outpost with such a difficult reputation as

Judea could have a capital like Caesarea! Of course the Jews consider Jerusalem their capital, and it is probably a very judicious choice to keep the bulk of our personnel removed from the center of their religious activities. But the city is a masterpiece of gleaming marble. As I understand, the city was initiated by the first Herod, who had the bad habit of murdering his wives and sons, but nevertheless was a genius with stone, to which numerous edifices in Judea will attest, including the great temple in Jerusalem.

About eight months ago, I was standing in the palace that Herod built which fronts the circular breakwater (an accomplishment in itself!). The occasion was a trial; the first that Festus was to administer—a very unusual trial—and one that would affect me more than I could possibly have imagined at the time. From my vantage point adjacent to the rostrum, I could see out the arched windows beyond the breakwater to the small whitecaps swelling and dipping in the summer sun. My thoughts, quite frankly, Uncle, were on a chestnut stallion in the stables, that had become a favorite of mine. Before the transition in government, I was able to take a spirited ride along the coast almost daily, and I was looking forward to the day when all the ceremony was over so I could resume a more idyllic existence.

(I know, dear Uncle, that you have hopes of my following you in the senate, but I am afraid my disposition has never been suited for political life.) Anyway, I was standing there in full dress, dreaming of the chestnut's hooves slinging sand and salt water as we raced along.

While in this gentle reverie, a motley assortment of convicts was trotted before Festus, the stale residue of the former governor's inefficient jurisprudence. *But my attention was arrested by one particular prisoner, a Jew, a man of small stature who was being accused by a somber group of fellow Jews of some sort of religious heresy. . . . . I say my attention was arrested by the man. Why? I'm not sure. But there was something almost regal in his deportment (although he was in chains and was rather scruffy, having spent two years in the dungeon because of Felix's irresolution). Little did I know at the time how well I would get to know this little heretic (one of the nicer things he was called by his vehement accusers).*

*It was an interesting sight to watch the somber accusers railing at the prisoner (his name is Paul) while he, on the other hand, seemed quite oblivious to the entire proceedings. It became obvious to anyone observing that Festus and the Jews had struck a prior agreement to have the trial moved to Jerusalem and this particular arraignment was to serve no purpose other than to give that agreement a legal veneer. No doubt his accusers had some plans of their own for the move. (Oh, Terentius, if we Romans ever marry our ideals to our actions, then we will be as great as we claim to be!)*

*However the prisoner thwarted everyone's plans for him by appealing to Caesar! He was, to everyone's surprise, a citizen of the empire! Of course, Festus had no other choice but to grant the appeal (which was very disconcerting, to say the least, to the Jewish religious leaders).*

*Nevertheless, plans were formulated to send Paul to Rome (along with several others whose fates were not so uncertain, whose final moments of life were appointed to give a sick pleasure to the crazed mobs attending what we so nobly refer to as the "games"). But the final plans were to be deferred until later, because Festus had just learned that his* brother-in-law, "King" Agrippa, was planning his official visit to Caesarea to welcome the new governor, and all efforts were channeled toward providing a proper reception.

Several days later Agrippa and his consort/sister did in fact arrive in Caesarea. Do not think, dear Uncle, that you in Rome have a monopoly on decadence, for in this region the "king" has added incest to the other vices—not the least of which vices is gluttony, as was evidenced in the four-day reception honoring Festus. It would have compared favorably with almost any such occasion in Rome— there were hams, chickens, pigeons, racks of lamb, roasted boar, several varieties of fish, ripe apples and grapes, mushrooms, sprouts, pears and chestnuts, and a number of other delicacies, all washed down with limitless amounts of Spanish wine. It was a memorable feast, dear Uncle, and though I ordinarily pride myself on being a temperate man, my stomach suffered much for my lack of moderation.

However, during the final day of this extravagant epicurism, as brother and brother-in-law lay on their couches gorging themselves, I had an opportunity to be privy to a conversation (accented by a chorus of satiated belches) which reverted back to the prisoner I have previously mentioned. As I recall, Agrippa had jested that the two of them would soon be as gross as the departed Felix if they long continued in such revelry. Festus laughed heartily at that suggestion, and then he grew serious and thoughtful. "There is a certain man," he said, "left a prisoner by Felix; and when I was at Jerusalem, the chief priests and elders of the Jews brought charges against him, asking for a sentence of condemnation upon him. But I answered them that it is not the custom of the Romans to hand

109

over any man before the accused meets his accusers face to face and has an opportunity to make his defense against the charges. And so after they had assembled here, I made no delay, but on the next day took my seat on the tribunal and ordered the man to be brought. And when the accusers stood up, they began bringing charges against him not of such crimes as I was expecting; but they simply had some points of disagreement with him about their own religion and about a certain dead man, Jesus, whom Paul asserted to be alive. And being at a loss of how to investigate such matters, I asked whether he was willing to go to Jerusalem and stand trial there on these matters. But when Paul appealed to be held in custody for the emperor's decision, I ordered him to be kept in custody until I send him to Caesar."

Agrippa was very studious for a moment before he responded to Festus' little discourse, and I had the impression that he had heard of this Christ-cult before. (Those who worship Jesus call him the Christ, as I was to learn later.) Then, very seriously, he responded, "I would like to hear the man myself," and it was agreed that the prisoner would be brought up the very next day.

Uncle, there are a least three things you need to understand concerning the proceedings at court.

First, the Jews take their religion very seriously. In fact, their religion dominates their lives. As you know, I, as well many in the army, perform some perfunctory sacrifices for Mithras because the cult encourages and inculcates those characteristics such as manliness and courage, which are essential for a well-trained fighting force. However, with the Jews it is quite a different matter—they seem to think of little else.

Second, Paul is not some backwoods religious

fanatic as you might suppose after reading only what I have written so far. On the contrary, Paul is a well-educated man, having received his classical education at the great university in Tarsus (a fact I learned from his companion Luke, a doctor; Paul seems unwilling to talk of anything that happened prior to his conversion to the Christ-cult).

And finally, concerning the resurrection of the Christ, it would be important for you to know that this is an event to which Paul is not alone in his attestation. There seems to have been quite a number of those who were supposed witnesses of the occurrence, some of whom are still alive, and pockets of followers have sprung up all over. In fact there are several of the believers (as many of them call themselves) within the ranks here in Caesarea.

(The worship of this Christ among the troops has not been discouraged, because it has seemed to have no harmful effect on the troops who are engaged in it; in fact their precepts require them to be obedient to those in authority and to be absolutely honest— qualities rare enough in even the best armies!)

Late the next day when everyone had reasonably recovered from the revelry of the previous days, amid an excess of pomp and ceremony (more than one of us winced when those intolerable trumpets were blown—adequate proof that wine remains in a man's brain long after it is drained from his bladder), the prisoner was indeed brought up again. And this time the auditorium was packed with people—those of us of the Roman administration as well as the prominent citizens of Caesarea whom Festus had invited.

Festus made a short introductory speech explaining the appeal made by the prisoner, but professing that he was at a loss to attach any particular charge to the prisoner's account. He summed it up

111

in quite inescapable logic: ". . . Therefore I have brought him before you all and especially before you, King Agrippa, so that after the investigation has taken place, I may have something to write. For it seems absurd to me in sending a prisoner, not to indicate also the charges against him."

At that point he yielded the floor to Agrippa, who indicated to Paul that he could speak in his own behalf.

Paul's manacles and chains rattled as he made a gesture with his hands, a mannerism I was to witness scores of times in the succeeding months. . . . (If Festus thought the absence of a proper charge was absurd, think of the necessity of keeping a small middle-aged man in chains, while surrounded by forty armed officers of the Roman army!)

If Paul had been somber and withdrawn in his previous appearance in court, he was now animated and calculating. He held the population of the auditorium in his manacled hands for the next few minutes as he made his defense. His presentation was clear and precise, punctuated with rattling gesticulations, and it was the audience, not the prisoner who was captive:

"In regard to all the things of which I am accused by the Jews, I consider myself fortunate, King Agrippa, that I am about to make my defense before you today; especially since you are an expert in all customs and questions among the Jews; therefore I beg you to listen to me patiently. . . .

"All Jews know my manner of life from my youth up, which from the beginning was spent among my own nation and at Jerusalem. Since they have known about me for a long time previously, they should be willing to testify that I lived as a Pharisee according to the strictest sect of our

waving the peacock fans over the incestuous royals. For Paul had wounded us with the cruellest weapon of all—his words. (Do not the strongest men always war with words and ideas?) Indeed, as I was to learn, Paul's mind is sharper than the steel I carry on my hip, and he, the defenseless one, had rendered us defenseless.

The obviously troubled Agrippa huddled with Festus and his advisers and the determination was made that although Paul was innocent of any crime, because he had appealed to Rome, there was no other choice than he would go to Rome. Agrippa's face was still red and his composure shaken when he turned back to the bandy-legged Jew. "You have appealed to Rome—to Rome you will go."

The next day I learned I was to have charge of a group of prisoners destined for Rome. (All except Paul were destined to provide with their own blood a few minutes entertainment for the frenzied crowd. For the whole of the journey I could not face one of those unfortunates—guilty as they no doubt were—without visualizing him as an ashen corpse being dragged out of the arena, while a dutiful attendant faithfully raked sand over his still-warm blood.)

I had eight of these poor fellows plus Paul. (All except Paul were chained to the mast below. Paul wore only a symbolic length of chain around his neck.) Because summer was fading quickly, I made plans to leave immediately. Two days later I had secured a small Adramyttium coaster bound for her home port. When she was properly fitted and stocked, we began to take the prisoners aboard.

Paul was on the pier saying his good-byes to a group of friends, when I saw that sweep of the hands, that rhetorical gesture so characteristic of him. . . . Terentius, do not think me presumptuous when I say I think I know something of leader-

115

ship. Having been born into a ruling family and having served in the Roman army for more than six years, I realize there are men who can never lead other men, while some men lead as naturally as they breathe or sleep. As I watched that small aggregation of souls on the dock, I noticed that there was something in their posture, in their deportment, that made me realize that the focus of the group was Paul. How did he command such authority? Certainly not by size! And he did not lead merely by education—for Apollos and Luke both were educated men as well. (I granted Luke permission to accompany Paul, as well as another Greek, Aristarchus, who although he was not a slave, voluntarily performed the function of Paul's man-servant on the trip.)

We weighed anchor on a cloudless day, the last week of August. For the next two weeks we crept along the coast northward and found our way into a wide river mouth at Myra, a comfortable port with a number of ships lying in harbor. We then embarked on a late-sailing Alexandrian grain ship whose owner was hopeful of fetching a higher price for his cargo in the Bay of Naples, because of the lateness of the year. The ship was designed for maximum tonnage, certainly not beauty or speed, but she was well-built and there were 276 of us who boarded that early autumn morning.

We made slow passage those first few days, bucking the northwesterlies, and each night we by necessity had to anchor until daybreak. During these days I got to know the physician, Luke, whom I mentioned earlier. He is quite an alert and interesting fellow and was constantly asking the pilot, in a polite and unobtrusive way, about the ship's progress; and these responses he dutifully recorded in a log of our journey.

One morning after I had consulted with the pilot and the ship's owner about the winds (they were hopeful of a shift in the wind's direction that would give us a favorable slant toward Italy), I engaged the physician in conversation. One of the more interesting things he mentioned was that he was in the process of writing an account of the life of their Christ (his given name was Jesus). He himself had never seen this Jesus in person, but he had talked with a number of people who had, and he had collected a great amount of information from those eyewitnesses, which he was turning into a history of the life of Jesus.

Soon we came into the port of Cnidus, put in new provisions, and since the headwinds remained constant, the pilot decided    drop down below Crete rather than to pu  ue our original intention of running straight through the Aegean Islands. The prevailing northerlies, which, according to the pilot, usually had subsided by this time of the year, pushed us briskly down underneath the islands where we found some relief from the steady north wind. We were fearful of being thrown farther south to Libya, but we were able to cast anchor in a poor harbor deceptively named Fair Havens.

The ship's owner was in turmoil at this juncture for he was beginning to lose hope that he would be able to reach Italy with his cargo before winter. The pilot concurred with the general opinion that winter weather had set in sooner than usual this year and that it would be wise to make plans for the winter and plan to catch the first favorable winds of spring.

Because I had some serious questions about the suitability of the harbor for wintering, I decided to convene a conference to discuss our options. I included Paul and Luke, the two Christ-followers, in

117

the discussion because both had done extensive travel throughout the Mediterranean. The pilot informed us that there was only one acceptable winter harbor on the southern coast of Crete, that being Phoenix, which lay to the northwest across the gulf, only one good day's sailing away.

Paul listened attentively to the discussion, but said nothing until it seemed all were concurrent in the opinion to avail ourselves of the first southerly wind to push us to Phoenix; then he spoke somberly like some dour prophet: "The ship is doomed." He stood and left the cabin.

I must admit, Uncle, I was more affected by this grave appraisal of our situation than a Roman soldier should have been. He did not try to change our mind or give any reasons for his dismal foreboding; he merely announced it as a matter of fact and then, like some bit actor in a Roman play, who, having delivered his few lines, left the stage. The amazing thing was . . . I believed him! But having no basis for remaining in that unsuitable harbor, I had no choice but to take the advice of the pilot and owner (and everyone else on board) and order the ship to stand ready for the first southerly wind, then make for Phoenix.

The next morning, as if to dispute Paul's conviction, a gentle wind came whispering up from Africa, and within minutes, we were under sail, hugging the coastline and making fair progress to Phoenix.

But, dear Uncle, if there are gods of the seas, they are cruel and capricious, for they tricked us into weighing anchor that October morning. The sun had not even crawled over our heads when the sail began to sag and droop. Every eye on board watched as the sail faltered in a moment of uncertainty; we all watched as it hung limp for a second, then quivered like some mortally wounded beast trying to stand, and then collapsed again. At that moment I felt the breeze across my face and watched in horror as the sails filled—the wind was from the north!

The shift was so sudden that it jerked the steering paddles from the hands of the helmsman. The ship turned with the wind and in a matter of seconds we were blown hundreds of yards away from land. The pilot and the sailors reacted quickly to lower the yard and shorten the sail, and soon the ship was under control, but the wind was mounting and we were drifting to the southwest— away from Crete!

The sea turned into foaming whitecaps as the wind poured over the mountains. Then I heard the word that strikes fear in the heart of every seafarer—"Euraquilo!" The great northeaster, the most dangerous wind in the Mediterranean, had arisen suddenly and was funneling down over the Cretan mountains with incredible fury.

After some hours of this furious storm, we sighted a rocky island, and by the great skill of our pilot, we slipped between two rocky islets and temporarily found a degree of relief from the storm. At the pilot's request I instructed my men to bring on deck the ship's lifeboat, while the sailors were engaged in a crucial task—wrapping the ship with cable-laid ropes. (The imminent danger was that the grain might start to swell with the moisture, putting intolerable pressure on the ship's hull.) The ropes, tightened by a windlass, helped relieve that pressure. At that moment I saw Paul, assisting my men, hoist the boat, and for a second my eyes caught his. I was surprised at two things: there was no condemnation in his eyes, and more surprisingly, neither was there any fear!

Then, because the pilot was afraid we were in danger of running up on the rocks, he set up a storm sail, let out the sea-anchor, and we drifted slowly away from that rocky outcropping. The gale persisted with consistent force, but we were at least able to control our drfit.

Dear Uncle, I will spare you the monotonous details of the succeeding two weeks. Suffice it to say that the next day we jettisoned the cargo. The following day we threw any unessential tackle overboard, and we settled in for what seemed an interminable period of constant swaying and seasickness.

There was little that could be done, and the days were hardly distinguishable from the nights. Our skin was scraped raw from the salt water; the odor of the bilge was intolerable; and men clung to the rails retching miserably.

At night our universe was reduced to little more than the span of a man's arm, and during the day a ghastly gray light prevailed, which extended our world only a few feet beyond the edge of the ship. The wind and the sea mounted a furious attack, driving our breath back into our throats.

Only once during our ordeal did I see the moon, and then for only a few fleeting seconds, as it slid through the sheets of clouds like a frightened demon, hastening from the scene of our torment.

This too-real nightmare proceeded for two weeks, and the ship's population drifted (just as the ship) into a gloomy sense of despair.

When this depression was at its worst and none of us had eaten anything substantial for days (the ship's galley fire had been closed on the first day of the storm), and many of us were quietly hoping for a quick death to end the tedious torture we were undergoing, Paul stood up and made a plea for us to take courage. According to him, he had had some sort of vision and we were all to be saved, but the ship was going to be lost.

There were those among us, who, if they had had the necessary energy after our exhausting ordeal, would have tossed the opinionated Jew overboard. Others simply dismissed his rantings about his god as that of a fanatic who had been pushed beyond his breaking point in the monotonous misery of the past two weeks. But I saw the piercing eyes of that self-styled prophet, and I tell you, my uncle, there was a clarity and a certitude there that was not of a madman.

During the midnight watch that evening, whispers ran through the sailors on duty as their instincts told them we were approaching land. Soundings were taken and the water was indeed shallowing quickly. When the pilot heard the boom and sizzle of breakers crashing, he ordered the anchors to be thrown out from the stern and to lay in wait until we could assess the situation in the morning.

As I stood there on the deck trying to catch sight of the shore through the murky darkness, Paul's voice was suddenly in my ear: "Unless these men remain in the ship, you yourselves cannot be saved." Like some silent specter that materializes out of the air, the salt-crusted prophet was at my side, pointing to the bow of the ship. I realized immediately what he was conveying: the cowardly sailors, under the pretense of laying out anchors, were about to lower themselves into the ship's boat! I sent six soldiers among them, and with cold steel at their necks they were influenced otherwise. I then ordered the ropes cut and the boat freed so there would be no further temptation for the sailors to abandon us, for certainly without them we would have been doomed.

As the day began to break, all the passengers began to assemble on the deck, and Paul went among them encouraging them all, distributing what remained of our soggy bread. Then he lifted his hands up and gave thanks to his god, and the passengers took some of the bread. The combination of Paul's encouragement, the food, and the sight of land served to allow a glimmer of hope to shine in our despair. I have often seen a campfire quenched by hours of torrential rain and seemingly cold, gray, and dead, revived and fanned to flames by the exposure to air of one small glowing ember deep under the soggy ash. Such is the human heart, my dear Uncle, and a new energy surged among us, as for the first time in many dreary days there was hope!

As the light increased, we saw we were just off a bay with a beach. The pilot quickly formulated a plan — we would drive the ship into the bay and with luck, onto the beach. The anchors were quickly cut loose, the small foresail lifted, and the ship surged forward into the bay. For some seconds everything looked good, but suddenly there was a crunching sound as the ship lurched and halted. We had struck a reef and were stuck fast! Panic seized the ship's passengers. The pounding waves were beginning to break up the ship's stern. The passengers were screaming in terror. I thought of the fickle sea gods again, and how we had been betrayed two weeks earlier. My captain, according to standing orders, was about to decapitate the prisoners, but I stayed his hand. Then I commanded those who could swim to go ahead and jump overboard, and for those who couldn't to follow with anything that would float.

Within a matter of minutes we were all in the foaming sea. Fortunately there was no shortage of planks, for the ship was splintering quickly. There were shrieks of terror and fright in the middle of the sea spray. Even some of my most seasoned men had been reduced to screaming idiots by the sudden turn of events. In the midst of this confusion I caught a glimpse of Paul, floating on a piece of ship's timber, those piercing eyes set on the shore, resolute as ever, and from all appearances, oblivious to the fury and confusion around us, simply bobbing up and down with the waves as if he could traverse the whole Mediterranean in that fashion! Luke, the physician, was close beside, clutching his precious papers.

In a few moments my feet touched ground, a thrill ran through my body! I had despaired of ever being on firm ground again. I clamored onto the beach like a madman and for a moment lay there facedown in the sand, exulting in the earth. I then organized the soldiers to help a few stragglers ashore and then we took a head count: to my amazement, all 276 of the passengers and crew were safe on land!

We learned from some natives we were on the island of Malta, and the hospitable Maltese were kind enough to build a fire. (Later it was reported that Paul was bitten by a viper as he gathered wood for this fire, but he simply shook the creature into the fire! I was not witness to the event, but the local populace later treated Paul with great respect. Their language was some Semitic tongue and Paul spoke with them in his native language, which, no doubt enhanced his position.)

We were able to secure fairly decent lodgings on the island and we settled in for a rather dreary winter, relieved somewhat by a series of long conversations with Paul and Luke.

Do you think it strange that I would seek out the

123

prisoners for discourse? I tell you it was refreshing to speak with men of education and character for a change. Did I say speak with? I must amend that. One does not speak with Paul. One listens to Paul. But Luke, the doctor, is an engaging, cheerful person, with a quick mind, and he and I spent many hours around our quarters talking of many things, but especially about his religion. As I mentioned, he has undertaken the writing of a chronology of the life of the Christ.

Two particular things concerning the Christ caught my attention: his birth and his death. His birth was in simple surroundings—a stable, according to Luke, uncluttered by the attendant trappings and pomp one might expect from so momentous an occasion. Likewise, his death was particularly ignominious—on one of our Roman crosses. "What was his crime?" you will ask. I can only respond: he told the truth. And do not think that so strange a crime, Uncle, for you very well know that many in Rome would die if they allowed themselves to be honest.

You no doubt will ask, "How can Paul and Luke worship someone whose birth and death were so inauspicious?" But as I came to realize, it is not the birth and death of Jesus that is absurd. No! It is Rome that is absurd—and every other culture that worships earthly power and its manifestations. After understanding the crucifixion of Jesus, I think I can never take worldly power seriously. Here was the one who was the power of God and yielded himself for his followers. When I understood this simple truth, dear Uncle, all my festering contempt for worldly pleasures, especially those enhanced and propagated by "the glory that is Rome," erupted.

You know well how I worshiped Rome. Everything seemed clear and indisputable when I was younger—I would be part of the cadre of troops that would bring "Rome's glory" to the world. But after slashing my sword through the necks of dozens of defenders, and having surveyed a battlefield when the stench of death hung like a noxious cloud on the earth, I am no longer sure that all issues are decided by the might of an army.

You will then ask me "Are you a Christian, Julius?" and I will not know how to answer. A good soldier, I have been taught, always makes his decisions based on his available choices. What are my choices? I certainly no longer worship Rome. . . . Rome, with its grotesque mobs seeking newer and more inventive ways to slaughter helpless men. . . . Rome, whose emperor and leaders act like animals and proclaim themselves to be gods. No, I once worshiped Rome, but no longer.

How proud I was the day I received my commission! As we stood there, Rome's finest youth, drawn swords shimmering in the sunshine, we were to be the ones to bring the glory of Rome to all the heathen nations. What an absurdity as I think of it now—we brought no glory—only death! And those who commissioned us, the Senate of Rome, given to no glory except glorifying self-indulgence (with only a few exceptions such as yourself, noble Uncle), how could they expect us to propagate anything except the seed of Rome, which is ostentation, excessive luxury, and pathetic obsession with the games—not glory! No, my uncle, Rome is dying, caving in on itself, stupefied by its own vanity, its approaching death evident in the insane slobberings of those attending the games. In fact, it is dead already. Some would say that Rome is growing, enlarging its borders, extending its influence. Perhaps. But I have seen more than one corpse lying on a battlefield swelling grotesquely before rotting away. Such is Rome, I believe, bloated with its own putrefaction, distended with its own corruption, swollen with its own spoilage, its carcass supported by the processes of death — not life — awaiting only further decomposition to finally fall in on itself.

Yes, I think Rome is already dead. Perhaps it died the day the first emperor designated himself as one of the deities.

Yes, my uncle, I will admit I feel a certain enchantment with the teachings of the prophet from Galilee, for I can still hear those sublime words Luke read to me: "Do not be anxious for your life, as to what you shall eat; nor for your body, as to what you shall put on. For life is more than food, and the body than clothing . . . but seek God's kingdom, . . . for where your treasure is there will your heart be also."

But am I a Christian? you ask. And I still do not know. Whether one of my temperament and attitude could ever conform to the moral ideas taught by Jesus, I don't know. Certainly I would prove to be no asset to the group, and yet, the precepts expounded by the Messiah are so pure and clean and true, it is to me like finding an exquisite jewel in a bucket of common gravel.

I can only say this: I no longer believe in the common assumptions of our culture — that by expanding our empire we will be greater; that by improving our position in life we will be better off; or that by increasing our wealth we will be happier. These notions I reject, and find it rather amusing that I ever accepted them. I now believe there is a "kingdom of God" and that it is a kingdom of the spirit, not of the flesh. As Rome decays in the dry rot of its own indulgence, I can only hope that in some way I can be a citizen in that new kingdom.

I know you too well, Uncle. Right now you are thinking: "Julius is fatigued. The terrible passage has taken its toll on him. When he comes here I will allow him to rest and in a few weeks he will be the same as before."

There is some truth in your assumptions. I am fatigued. And I am looking forward to being with you and lounging in your gardens. I am sure the terebinth and the lilacs are in bloom now, and I want to breathe deeply those blossoming aromas. And, no doubt, you will have luscious fruit from the provinces, and we will sit in the warm sun and I will tell you of Judea and you will tell me of all my cousins—which have married, which are prospering, and which are disgracing the family by some scandalous behavior!

Yes, Uncle, I look forward to our time together, but do not think I will be the same—I think I will never be the same again. But I must close my narrative. . . .

When winter was over and the island began to awake to the warmth of the spring, I secured our passage on an Alexandrian ship that had wintered on Malta. We had an uneventful trip on this last leg of the journey and in a few days, the Italian coast was sighted and a great cheer went up from the passengers. We skirted along the coast, saw the lazy curl of smoke above Vesuvius, and we have now stopped in Puteoli where I am writing this letter.

127

My plan is to rest here for a week and then make our way overland to Rome.

I look forward to seeing you face to face.

Your immediate nephew,
Julius

Jim took the Bible and went to his room. He sat in the tattered old chair in the corner of the cinder-block building. Adjusting the dilapidated lamp, he settled in to read Luke's Gospel. The first two chapters were fairly familiar to him, he realized, as they would be to almost anyone who celebrated Christmas.

"And in the same region there were some shepherds staying out in the fields, and keeping watch over their flock by night. And an angel of the Lord suddenly stood before them, and the glory of the Lord shone around them; and they were terribly frightened. And the angel said to them, 'Do not be afraid; for behold, I bring you good news of a great joy which shall be for all the people; for today in the city of David there has been born for you a Savior, who is Christ the Lord.' "

In chapter three he found an example of the

gospel being "rooted in history," as Dr. Crawford put it:

"Now in the fifteenth year of the reign of Tiberius Caesar, when Pontius Pilate was governor of Judea, and Herod was tetrarch of Galilee, and his brother Philip was tetrarch of the region of Ituraea and Trachonitis, and Lysanias was tetrarch of Abilene, in the high priesthood of Annas and Caiaphas, the word of God came to John, the son of Zacharias, in the wilderness."

As he read, small pieces of the narrative, particularly the words of Jesus, flashed across his consciousness in a moment of recognition:

*"Do not be anxious for your life, as to what you shall eat; nor for your body, as to what you shall put on. For life is more than food, and the body than clothing."*

Like the seeds of the open field affix themselves to the way-passer, these stubborn bits of Scripture were attached to his consciousness—always unintentionally. An occasional sermon he had heard, an inscription on a church, a magazine article read in an airport—his spiritual education, like his life, had been intermittent and fitful, without purpose or direction.

*"Whoever does not carry his own cross and come after Me cannot be My disciple."*

But for the most part, the words he was reading were unfamiliar. He read hungrily, expectantly. Never had he known such an acute awareness or his concentration so focused.

*"Truly I say to you, whoever does not receive the kingdom of God like a child shall not enter it at all."*

Jim continued to read Luke's Gospel. For

the first time he understood the flow of events in the life of Christ—the teaching and healing ministries, the burgeoning multitudes that followed him, the conflict with the religious leaders . . .

"*. . . woe to you, you whitewashed tombs . . ."*

The entry into Jerusalem, the sham of a trial . . .

"*And they began to accuse Him, saying, 'We found this man misleading our nation and forbidding to pay taxes to Caesar, and saying He Himself is Christ, a King.' "*

The crucifixion . . .

"*And when they came to the place called The Skull, there they crucified Him and the criminals, one on the right and the other on the left."*

And the resurrection . . .

"*Why do you seek the living One among the dead? He is not here, but He has risen."*

Jim closed the book.

Out in the still night a jackal bayed an eerie note—the only sound in a camp that had long been asleep.

Jim realized how little he had known of the life of Christ and how radically Luke's portrayal of Him differed from his own preconception. Here was not the 'gentle Jesus, meek and mild,' or the weak, emaciated, almost effeminate character he had seen portrayed on a crucifix, but a real man, unafraid of conflict, who, in every circumstance knew Himself and His mission perfectly. *Oh, to know some of that certainty myself.*

Jim put the Bible on the table and stretched out on the bed, pulling the covers over him. As he lay there, for the first time that he could remember in his adult life, a tear ran across his face. A whole flood of emotions he did not understand washed over him as the one tear gave way to more. He began sobbing uncontrollably as all his pent-up emotions came pouring out, and he cried himself to sleep.

He had slept only a few hours when he heard the Jeep screech to a halt outside the building. A door slammed and he heard Kavakis's voice in the room next to his: "Professor, Professor, the scroll has been stolen!"

The lone rat slipped noiselessly down the thick rope of the anchored ship *Saggita,* an Egyptian vessel that had taken on grain at Carthage.

The Constantinople harbor lay calm and tranquil below a three-quarter moon that silhouetted the ships that lay at harbor. The sound of the small waves rippling against the pier and the lazy groan of the ships' timbers as the vessels rubbed against their moorings meshed into a lethargic rhythm, the only breach of that rhythm being the punctuated outbursts of a small group of sailors and wharf derelicts huddled around a kettle fire, sharing ribald stories and a bottle of wine.

As the rat reached the dock, she paused for a second to sniff the air for any danger with her pink nose. Driven by her instincts, she knew she must find a safe place to bear her young, and the urgings of her body told her it would not be long before she would deliver.

All day she had hidden in a cavity of the ship's hull as the sailors had unloaded the cargo, depriving her not only of food, but of adequate shelter. After the ship was unloaded and darkness came, she had waited patiently for several hours before she sought a suitable place to deliver her babies.

Now as she stood erect, sniffing the air, hidden behind the wharf's pilings, she examined her possibilities: the storage buildings were only about sixty feet away, but the pier between the two points was essentially open and offered little protection. Still she knew she had no other choice; the compelling pain in her body made her realize the birth of her offspring was imminent.

Testing the air one final time, the rat dropped to four feet and began to slip along the edge of the pier farthest from the men. Below her, the dark water gurgled around the pilings as the tiny waves crested and broke.

It happened so quickly that she did not know what occurred: a sharp noise, an agonizing pain in her hindquarters, a sickening fall, a splash, then dark, cold water surrounded her. She struggled to the surface and heard the voice of a man.

"Ha! I hit it! I hit the filthy rat!" the scraggly looking man said as he peered over the rail, wine bottle in his hand.

"Proclus, bring the bottle back and quit your babbling," one of the sailors sitting around the fire said.

"I tell you I hit it," Proclus said. "Vile rats— they eat more on one voyage than all the hands."

"Proclus," another said, "you couldn't hit the ocean if we stood you on the edge of the pier!"

A chorus of laughter followed.

"Even if he were sober!" another added.

More laughter.

"I tell you I hit it," Proclus said, irritated. "And I hope the dirty rodent drowns." He swore as he tried to focus his bloodshot eyes on the black water below.

"I wish I could kill every one of those filthy beggars. All night I hear them scurrying around my feet when I'm trying to sleep."

"Why don't you get a proper house," one said, winking at the others, "instead of sleeping in that pile of thatch? Perhaps you could get an appointment as a member of the Praetorian Guard. You could be in charge of protecting Justinian from rats!" The group of men snorted in laughter.

Proclus cursed at his detractors. "I tell you I hit it . . . probably drowned."

Proclus was partly right. The lead weight he had cast at the silhouette on the pier had skipped off the planking into the left hip of the expectant rat, knocking her, careening, to the water below. But she did not drown. Her left hind leg was crushed, but she was able to swim to one of the pilings and drag herself up to the storage buildings above. There she found refuge in a pile of salvaged timbers, the rotting remains of a broken-up ship's boat. She managed to gather some discarded fish nets to form a rude nest for her offspring. From the smell of the air she was certain there was not only available food in the building but also other rats as well. Her body convulsed and she gave a whimper. The babies were coming.

Proclus the sailor, maligned by his mates, would never know how close he came to changing the course of history, for the female rat that deserted the ship *Saggita* on a spring night of A.D. 542, carried in her body the force that would crumble the already beleaguered Byzantine Empire.

"Why? Why?" Justinian hung his head over the map. He was sixty years old and had been emperor for fifteen years, and before that he had been the real power behind his uncle Justin's throne for nine years.

"Twenty-four years," he said, "and . . . *this!*" The emperor stood and walked around the table. His principal advisers, including Belisarius, his field general, were standing silently around the map.

In previous generations, the Mediterranean had been a Roman lake; every land touching its waters ruled by Rome. But now in the spring of 542, however, the map that Justinian looked at was far different from the one that Nero, Vespasian, or Domitian would have surveyed during their reigns.

Justinian turned back to the map. "Cursed Chosroes," he said, looking at the lands claimed by Persia. "May God have no mercy on his soul."

Chosroes the Persian was several years younger than Justinian, and although the two men had never met, Chosroes was the emperor's chief antagonist—and had been for thirty years. A hard and cruel man, Chosroes never fought a sustained war, or a war of conquest; plunder was his aim, and he knew the Roman garrisons could not effectively police the entirety of Asia Minor. Repeatedly his armies descended on the opulent Roman cities and carried away the cities' riches, leaving behind smoking ruins.

Two years earlier Chosroes had become more ambitious. His army had crossed the Euphrates, razed Sura, and marched toward the coast and Antioch. The six thousand Roman soldiers attached to the garrison had fled before the superior Persian forces. The Antioch citizens, however, had defended their city valiantly—but they were no match for a trained army. The Persians soon had broke through and begun a systematic massacre.

Justinian, plagued by problems in the East, could not afford to fight a war on the western front at the time and had capitulated to Chosroes's demands: five thousand pounds of gold for the Persian army to retreat!

Justinian winced as he thought of the ransom. He had paid it, but he had vowed to himself that he would have it back, along with the head of Chosroes on a pole. Now he was not so sure of that vow. "Order! There must be order!" Justinian shouted as he slammed his fist on the table.

The emperor looked at the map of Italy. Two hundred years previously Constantine had moved the Roman Empire's capital to the city he had built and named after himself. Rome, however, had been taken by the Visigoths in 410. Italy was still under Gothic administration when Justinian came to power, and even though the Goths had devised a system whereby Gothic military control would ensure the Roman way of life, Justinian was not content to allow the Germanic invaders to control the seat of the original Roman Empire. It was his destiny, he had decided, to restore the empire to its original bounds and glory. "I will again bring the glory of the Roman Empire to the world," he had told the cheering crowd on his inauguration day. And Rome was of the highest priority.

But now he was being threatened on all sides. "Too many fronts, too many enemies," he said vacantly. He looked at the kingdoms that fringed his borders—the Moors, Visigoths, Franks, Huns, Slavs, Persians, Arabs . . . and the list went on. The British Isles, France, Spain, in fact, all of northern Europe was no longer under the empire's control. Even Italy itself was contested.

". is my destiny," he said looking around the i m, "to restore the empire. And the empire c nnot be restored until Italy is ours. We must conquer the Goths, *then* we can turn our attention to the other borders."

Little did Justinian know that there was a hideous, invisible force at work in the sewers and dumps of the city that would render all plans and powers impotent.

"By the gods, mates, he's dead!"

A handful of wharf derelicts, plus a few sailors, gathered around the body of the man lying in the thatch next to the storage buildings. "It's Proclus," another said.

"He didn't die easy, did he?" one said. "Look at his face. And look at the thatch, how its all strewn around. He had a bad night of it, all right."

"And look at those splotches on his skin!" another said. "Think he got some bad grog?"

"I don't think so," one of the sailors said. "I saw eight men die of poison grog in Crete. They had a rough time of it, but they didn't have those black splotches."

"Well, whatever it was, it killed him, and someone needs to summon the authorities to bury him."

"It's strange," the youngest man said as they walked away.

"What's strange?" asked the sailor.

"Proclus," the man answered. "He was so alive just a few days ago. Remember last week when we gave him such a hard time about throwing at that rat? He was so alive then. . . . I know he was just a worthless old coot, but it makes me feel bad that we were on to him so hard."

"Don't feel bad, sonny. When you've seen as many die as I have, you get used to it. None of us has any assurance we'll take another breath, and that's a fact."

The death of a drunken derelict was not an event significant enough to warrant attention at the royal palace, but a few days later a report came to General Belisarius that a dozen men had died ghastly deaths in the harbor area, half of them sailors of the Imperial Navy. The next day the number of deaths doubled, and it more than tripled on the next. By the end of the week more than six hundred had died, primarily in the waterfront area, and news was all over the city that some strange disease had invaded Constantinople.

The subject was mentioned in the daily sessions of the emperor and generals in the great palace, but it was hoped that the malady would soon pass. However, when the death toll reached more than a thousand in one day, Justinian had the court physician summoned to give a report.

Ordinarily, one summoned to the emperor's court was required to stand to deliver his message, but when Justinian saw the doctor's condition, he ordered a stool for him to sit on. The doctor sat, his shoulders heavy. Although his eyes were red from lack of sleep, they were placid and serene. He spoke flatly and slowly, without emphasis, as though all his emotion had been spent.

"This past evening," the physician began, his eyes unfocused, "I attended the son of a nobleman, a young, virile boy of twenty years of age. The report I shall give will concern him particularly, however the description I shall give would fit the symptoms that have been reported in hundreds of other cases; in fact, as I attended the young man I could hear the screams of the dying in adjacent houses."

So the doctor relayed the course of the disease: fever and chills, fits of vomiting, large swelling lumps beginning in the groin and armpits that would erupt with blood and pus, dark purplish blotches appearing on the skin, and finally delirium and spasms of pain, ending in death.

By the end of June, the death toll reached more than five thousand a day. In the stifling heat of July, more than ten thousand per day died of the horrible plague.

Pandemonium reigned in the streets of Constantinople. The civil administration could not control the looters or maintain a system of burying the dead. The stench of death pervaded the city despite efforts to transport the bodies to empty buildings in the country. Many inhabitants of the city bolted their doors, refusing entrance to even their closest friends. The regular food supply was disrupted as farmers refused to bring their merchandise to the city. So, to the already calamitous circumstances was added a severe shortage of food.

The plague was most severe in the poorer sections, where the greatest concentration of rats was located; for the disease was being transferred from rats to humans. But even the noblest and richest were not exempt from the horror of the disease, and many high-placed officials succumbed.

In early August a rumor reached the streets which was later confirmed—the emperor had the plague!

Belisarius and Photius sat at the emperor's bedside, waiting for him to awaken. Except for his labored breathing, Justinian could have been mistaken for a corpse—his face was ashen and dark blotches were visible all around his throat.

The general and his stepson had been waiting at the bedside for nearly an hour, ever since they had received word that Justinian wanted to speak to them. A slave stood

141

behind the bed, monotonously waving a palm branch over the monarch's head. Occasionally Justinian, although asleep, would twitch in pain. After several more minutes a pain hit Justinian that awakened him and doubled him over. Belisarius and Photius watched as Justinian writhed in pain, his hands clawing at the edge of his bed. After a short time the pain subsided, and the emperor strained to speak, his face glistening with sweat.

"Belisarius," Justinian said in a weak and hoarse voice.

"I am here, sire."

"And Photius?"

"He is here beside me," Belisarius answered. Photius leaned nearer so Justinian could see him. He was not Belisarius' true son, but the young man was deeply committed to his stepfather.

"I have a mission for you," Justinian rasped, struggling to raise himself on the bed.

"For which of us, sire?" Belisarius said.

"Photius. I can't spare you now, Belisarius— you must stay here. Photius, come closer."

As Photius stood and leaned over the bed, Justinian had a sudden spasm of coughing. When he was finished, he lay still and quiet, and for a moment, Photius was not sure whether he was still alive; but then Justinian opened his red, watery eyes and spoke.

"I made a vow," he said forcing the words out of his mouth.

Photius leaned closer, not comprehending what the emperor was saying, but not wanting to interrupt him.

"You must go to St. Catherine's for me. . . . See Bishop Menas. . . . I've already

spoken to him. He will tell you. . . . Be careful of Chosroes. . . . Must rest now. . . ."
The emperor slipped into a merciful unconsciousness. Belisarius checked his wrist to verify that there was still life in the emperor's body. He confirmed it to those attending him, then he and Photius rose to leave.

Once outside the palace, Photius asked, "What did he mean, Father, 'You must go to St. Catherine's'? Was he speaking of the monastery in the Sinai? Do you think perhaps he has. . . ."

"Lost his mind?" Belisarius asked. "I doubt it. I don't think those were the rantings of a madman. The plague *does* do strange things to men, however. Whatever the case, perhaps the bishop can enlighten us."

A few minutes later Photius and Belisarius were standing with Bishop Menas in the center of Santa Sophia, the Church of Holy Wisdom. Polished marble of every conceivable hue glittered as the afternoon sun penetrated the ring of windows around the dome one hundred feet above their heads.

Santa Sophia was one cornerstone of Justinian's master plan for the empire: The empire he would restore would be God's instrument of bringing Christianity to the whole world. Constantinople was to be both the new Rome and the New Jerusalem and as such, the city had to have a point of convergence, where the political and religious realms, the earthly and heavenly realms, could intersect. Such a place was Santa Sophia.

The bishop's voice echoed off the gleaming marble. "Yes, Justinian made a vow," he said. "You may recall his building the monastery at

Mt. Sinai. It is called St. Catherine's. At the time of its completion, Justinian promised to invest it with some of the church's riches—artwork, manuscripts, carvings, carpets, embroidery, and the like. He himself chose what he wanted to send. It is locked in a vault in the cellar. But the pressures of his administration, I'm afraid, have kept him from completing this vow."

"And now he is clearing his accounts," Belisarius said.

"Yes, it sounds like it. He called me to his side this morning to tell me of the mission he would assign you. Come :h me. I will show you the vault."

Menas led them down a circular staircase at the rear of the church. Opening a massive door, he went in and lit several candles. Photius, when his eyes were adjusted, walked around the room examining the treasures. In one corner lay a stack of tapestries, rolled up and covered. There was a series of stacks of icons, colorful portraits of the saints, arranged by size. There were carved screens for altars, silver plates, heavily embroidered priestly vestments, a great stack of manuscripts thickly bound, and a few items in scroll form.

"Where is all this from?" Photius asked.

"Rome," Menas answered. "When Constantine came here to form a second capital, he brought many of the church's artifacts with him."

Photius picked up a few of the books and held them up to the light to examine the exquisite and colorful artwork on the pages. He then picked up a scroll encased in cedar, and was admiring it when Menas spoke.

144

"The loss of this," he said, pointing around the room, "will certainly not deplete the church treasury, but it will be a welcome offering, I'm sure, to the monks at St. Catherine's. I'm afraid your assignment, Photius, is to deliver these goods to those monks." Photius replaced the scroll on the shelf. "I will leave to you and your father the logistics of arranging the journey—each of you is better equipped in that area than I. Justinian has made whatever resources you may need available to you. One thing he kept repeating, 'He must be careful of Chosroes.' "

"Yes, he said the same thing this morning," Photius said, looking at his father.

"Well, God's mercy go with you."

Outside, Belisarius was explaining to his son what he thought was the best course of action. "You must leave quickly. Day after tomorrow should give you time to organize. Take only a handful of men. You must try to slip through Chosroes' armies—try to avoid a confrontation. Travel at night when you are near him and take great precaution. Oh, one other thing. When you depart, go a two-day's journey, find a secluded spot, and camp there five days. Do not proceed further until you are sure the party is free from the plague."

As the ferry pulled away from the shore, Photius waved good-bye to his stepfather. On board he had eight handpicked men, most of them young, about his own age. For this mission, age and experience would not be as essential as youthful energy. In addition to the eight soldiers and their horses, there were eight other beasts of burden and three slaves to handle them and the cargo. The bundles were securely attached to the animals' backs. Fortunately, the ferry across the strait—the narrow gap between Europe and Asia—took only a few minutes, for Photius was anxious to be clear of the populated areas as soon as possible.

The sun was only a promise below the eastern horizon as he looked back on the city, the dome of Santa Sophia gleaming in the early morning light. There was no indication of the scourge that was penetrating the city, yet again thousands would die this day, and thousands more the next.

Amazingly, Justinian was not among those who died, even though more than forty percent of the great city's population would be dead before the disease ran its course. He fully recovered from the disease and lived to rule the empire for twenty-three more years.

But although Justinian did not die with the plague, his dream of a new empire did. Constantinople, as well as the rest of the empire, would never recover from the devastation wrought upon it by the invisible enemy. The military, the civil administration, agriculture, and all other institutions were affected by the catastrophe. The Romans' own self-indulgence had weakened the empire; Goths, Lombards, Bulgars, Persians and a dozen others had hurt it; and eventually the armies of Mohammed would slay it. But it was the invisible bacillus that gutted the greatest empire the world had ever known and rendered it impotent.

Photius checked the train to be sure everything was in place, then he swung his leg

mountains. On the next day, as they neared the high passes, a man was sighted in the upper rocks—no doubt a lookout for a band of thieves; but they must have decided against risking an attack on such a virile-looking group with bows and swords displayed prominently, for the Romans continued their journey without incident.

The next two days they made very good time as they moved across the plains of Galatia, where the Apostle Paul had planted churches five centuries before.

Reaching the Cappadocian borders, they traded their horses for new ones. Volcanic dust and snow water combined to make this area the best pasture in the empire, and the finest horses, including a special breed of racing horses, were bred and raised there. Photius's young soldiers were enthused about their sleek, well-muscled mounts, and Photius had to admit that if it came to an issue of speed between them and the steeds of Chosroes' armies, they would be well-equipped.

When they reached the Cilician Gates the tax collector, an old man with a yellow beard, appraised them of the situation beyond: "It has been nearly two years since Chosroes destroyed Antioch. Took the young and healthy back to Persia. Killed all the others. Hasn't been much traffic through here since then. Only safe way to travel to Judea or Egypt has been by sea. That is, until this plague broke out. Seems to be much worse in the port cities, so I've been told."

Photius knew the truth of what the old man was saying. The port cities, for some reason,

149

had been hit hardest by the disease, and he knew that was the reason Justinian wanted the cargo to travel overland.

"Don't know what the world's coming to," the old man said, shaking his head. "But anyhow, you asked about Chosroes. Doesn't keep his armies in any one place very long. Doesn't really control any territory—just makes it impossible for our army to control it. He raided cities all around Antioch, then crossed back over the Euphrates to Persia. But he's back again, and according to what I've heard, keeps a close eye on the roads. A wise piece of advice for you, young man: Take your cargo and your young men and head back to where you came from —unless you want your head on the end of a Persian pole."

Photius thanked the man for his advice, and they made their way to a place about twenty miles north of Tarsus. The next morning they spoke to an old widow who lived alone in a crude hut. She had not seen the Persians in several weeks and figured they were further south, closer to Antioch. She, too, advised them to turn back. Photius thanked her for her concern and gave her a handful of silver coins. She was stunned at the small fortune and repeatedly kissed Photius' hands, loudly praising God all the time.

By the middle of the day, Photius found a thicket of heavy pines and told his men to rest for the afternoon.

There in a thick bed of pine needles, while some slept and others sharpened and resharpened their swords and arrow tips, Photius took out his map and evaluated his course of action.

They waited nearly two hours after sunset before emerging from the pine thicket. Photius adjusted the sword on his hip. He intended to avoid conflict if it were at all possible, but if a fight could not be avoided, he would prove himself a man even in the face of overwhelming odds—the son of Belisarius could do no less.

But the night proved uneventful. Stealthily and slowly they made their way over the rocky road. Not even venturing a whisper, they progressed silently through the night. Photius kept a constant watch on the rocks beside them, constantly anticipating the scream of a Persian soldier and a mad onslaught, but the only sound of the night was the steady clopping of the horses' hooves on the rocky ground.

Just as the sun began to cast an orange glow over the rocks beside them, Photius found a deep cleft in the cliffs to shelter them for the day. The trees were not as dense as those they had slept under the day before, but there was a sheer cliff at their back which would afford some protection. When the horses were tied and fed, and a guard posted, the weary men slept under the scrubby trees.

Late in the afternoon as Photius was poring over his map trying to determine how much territory they had covered, Sergius, one of his men, scurried from his watchman's post and said in an excited whisper: "I saw someone— up above!"

"Where?" Photius asked. He felt a lump rise in his throat and his pulse quicken.

"There!" Sergius said, pointing to a spot almost directly above them.

Photius scanned the outline of the rocks but could see no one. "How many were there?" he whispered.

"I only saw one."

"Tell everyone to act normally. Do not arouse suspicion. Keep all swords sheathed. Do you understand me?"

Sergius nodded.

"I will return in a few minutes," Photius said as he removed his sword. "Remember, tell everyone to act normally!"

Photius walked slowly through the scrub toward the face of the cliff. There was a small fissure slightly wider than a man's shoulders that opened into the granite wall. At the back of the fissure there was a slope of loose rock leading to the top. Photius quickly scrambled up the rocks like a leopard. He felt an incredible strength in his arms and legs; his mind was focused on what he would find in the gap above. Perhaps it was a single lookout. If so, maybe he could get behind him and subdue him before he could alert anyone else.

As he neared the top, he heard a horse's whinny and the sound of hooves. He emerged just in time to see the single horse and its rider ride off across the plateau.

When Photius returned to the campsite, the men were tense with anticipation, but before they could ask a question, he gave an order: "Gather firewood. Each of you—gather firewood."

The men looked at each other in disbelief. "But . . ." Sergius started.

"You heard me," Photius interrupted. "I want every dead limb you can find. We are going to have a blazing campfire tonight!"

The men looked at each other incredulously, but dispersed to follow Photius' command. By dark, a great pile of wood lay ablaze in the middle of the camp. One man was posted in the rocks above to watch, but everyone else was instructed to put swords and bows under their blankets and to wait.

His men were puzzled, but Photius thought his plan would give them the best chance of completing their mission and escaping alive—it all depended on how much the spy above them had seen. A quick dash to the south had been his first inclination, but that was ruled out when he saw the direction the spy rode—south. No doubt they would have been cut off farther down the road.

Yes, he was convinced his plan offered their best chance—*but would it work?* He could only wait and see.

Photius diligently tended the fire into the night. A great heap of orange coals lay at the base and the rising heat caused the leaves of the overhanging trees to flutter. Above those trees Photius could see the dying embers mix with a great host of stars in a motionless heaven. The unpredictable cracking of the fire was the only sound of the night. The men lay around sleeping, and Photius had begun to hope that the lone horseman he had seen was not a part of Chosroes' army. But his wishful thinking was killed when he heard his sentry scrambling down the crevice.

"Horses," the sentinel reported. Another of the men started to douse the fire but Photius stopped him.

"How many?" Photius asked.

"I couldn't see them," he answered, "but I

heard them. Must be hundreds."

Photius cocked his head to listen. A low, insistent rumble welled up into the night air. Horses' hooves! And the sentry's estimate was conservative.

"Sergius, come here," Photius said excitedly as he placed some more branches on the fire. "In Constantinople you had the bad habit of loitering around the circus watching those shoddy plays. We're going to see how well you've learned your dramatics; you're about to have the worst case of the plague that has ever been reported. Get your blanket and come over closer to the fire."

Sergius stood with a blank expression on his face for some seconds until he figured out Photius' intent.

"Get your blanket, man!" Photius repeated. "I need two men to tend the sick man. The rest of you, just remain still. And if this doesn't work. . ." he paused for a moment, "I want you to know that I die in good company."

Photius continued to add branches to the fire. It cast a great yellow light, illuminating the entire grove of trees.

The low rumble grew to a roar until there was a great clatter of hooves as the horses came to a stop. Photius stood in front of the fire and watched as one figure, then several, then dozens, stood on the rim above them peering down. He kicked Sergius who began to moan pitifully.

A voice came from above: "Hello, down there. Who are you?"

"Poor traders," Photius answered. "We are

taking black wool from Phrygia to Damascus. And who might you be, sir?"

"Chosroes, general of the armies of Persia, you impudent moron," came another voice, deep and harsh. Photius saw one figure step to the front of the column, "and I think you have gold and silver in those bags."

Sergius let out a great groan.

"You are welcome to inspect our meager goods," Photius answered. "And perhaps you might have some medicines for my poor servant—he has a fever and a strange swelling in his groin."

Sergius' groan reverberated throughout the canyon.

Photius watched the silhouettes on the rim of the cliff as this information passed through the ranks. He knew that the Persians had not been immune to the plague and that they would be familiar with the symptoms.

The only sound in the canyon was Sergius' low moaning.

"Perhaps you have a surgeon in your ranks," Photius shouted, "my poor servant is in great pain and. . . ."

"We have no medicines and no surgeons," the malevolent voice came back, and if you are not away from this place by morning, my archers will use you for target practice." With that, Chosroes turned, mounted his horse, and the great horde rode off.

"Keep up the charade," Photius whispered. "They may have left spies behind."

So for the next several hours they maintained their vigil over the agonizing Sergius, culminating in a fake burial in the shadows.

Before daybreak they departed the canyon leaving behind a great heap of gray ash and one freshly dug, but empty, grave.

By the middle of the morning the caravan sighted the Roman garrison at Apamea and they broke out into a gallop. That night there was a great celebration, much self-congratulations, and it was generally agreed, among much laughter and backslapping, that Sergius was destined for a great career on the Constantinople stage, and that there was no finer leader than Photius, the man who invited the armies of the awful Chosroes to his camp and then scared him off with only eight men at his side! It was a story to be retold over thousands of campfires in succeeding generations.

The Sinai lay three hundred miles farther south, but the land was secure. Neither Chosroes nor anyone else would dare enter the area of Samaria, Judea, or the Sinai. The artifacts, including the scroll, would make it to St. Catherine's.

Justinian's pledge was fulfilled.

Kavakis presided over the hastily called meeting. Dr. Crawford, Sarah, and Jim sat around a small table. Neat rows of labeled artifacts lay around them as Kavakis explained the situation: "Yosuf came into camp about half an hour ago. As nearly as I can tell from his report, the manuscript was stolen only two or three hours ago. At least three men broke into his grandfather's house and took the scroll. They banged the old man around a little bit but he's OK. In fact, as they left, he got his old blunderbuss and fired a parting shot. Whether or not he hit one of the thieves we don't know. But we need to quickly decide our course of action."

"What will they do with the scroll?" Jim asked.

"I don't think they will try to extract a ransom for it," the professor said. "I doubt if they're professional enough for that course of action. I wish they would sell it back to us. We could pay more than they could conceivably expect, and I suppose we could find some grounds for justifying our action—but I seriously doubt if that possibility has occurred to them.

"No," the professor continued, his face showing his anguish, "their most likely course of action is the one I fear most—no doubt they will cut the manuscript up and sell it piecemeal."

"It's happened before," Kavakis agreed. "Selling it a piece at a time solves the problem of dividing the loot; and it enables them to determine the going price by selling only a scrap. No doubt the price will go up with every piece sold."

"And the entire manuscript would *never* be recovered," the professor said morosely. "Scraps would be scattered all over the world, and some portions would be lost forever."

"That's why we must act quickly," Kavakis said. "I questioned a few of the workers and offered a reward for helping us find the scroll—I feel sure our missing worker is the key. One of our more trustworthy helpers came forward to identify the missing man. He is from Jericho—not a stranger to the law, according to our worker. I think our best bet is to alert the police in Jericho. They may know where to find him."

"Kavakis is right—it is our only chance," Dr. Crawford said to the others.

# 10

Constantine Tischendorf rode in the rear.

Ahead of him, barely visible in the dim shadows, were four more camels, three of which were ridden by a trio of Arab guides. The other of the humped animals was laden with supplies. Before them the Negev lay flat and trackless under the night sky. A few desert scrubs, hardly visible in the half light, dotted the hills, the only survivors of the sun-bleached soil.

Tischendorf settled into the lethargic rhythm of the camel. The motion and cadence would have driven lesser men mad. The constant, muscle-wrenching, monotonous motion was a rhythm centuries old, known to bands of nomads that had continually crisscrossed this austere land on camelback. But few Westerners were temperamentally equipped to adjust to many days in the hard saddle.

The train was headed southeast, parallel to

the axis of the arching hills. The route ahead of them was dry and austere and behind them the desiccated landscape differed in no way, save for the tracks of camel hooves in the crusty soil.

Tischendorf was a thin, bespeckled man, who in spite of the lurching motion of the camel, had the unruffled deportment of a scholar. This punishing journey was the third trek he had made across the great Negev during his long and distinguished career, and he knew in his bones that it would be his last. The last few nights as he had stretched out his aching body under the magnificent desert sky, he was certain that this was his final trip to the Sinai. He only hoped that this final trip would be successful.

Now fifty-four years old, the German scholar had not been a stranger to either success or tedious work. While he was still in his early twenties he had earned the nickname "the manuscript detective" for his work on the famous "Codex C." The ancient manuscript had been the object of scrutiny for several years. The difficulty of translation was due to Codex C being a *palimpsest*, literally meaning "scraped again." Some twelfth-century monk, suffering from a shortage of writing material, had erased the seven-hundred-year-old text (no doubt thinking he had a "better" manuscript at hand) and written on it a series of sermons by a Syrian saint by the name of Ephraem. The deciphering of the original text proved to bring nothing but frustration to other scholars, so it was turned over to the young German.

Tischendorf brought only two things to his

task: marvelous eyesight and inexhaustible patience. For three years he labored over the faint markings and was able to recover the original text. His translation was so accurate that modern ultraviolet lighting techniques served to authenticate his findings.

As a young man Tischendorf was a defender of the authenticity of the Bible in a period in which there were harsh attacks on the Scriptures, primarily from his own countrymen. He was convinced of the reliability of the New Testament and realized his contention could be authenticated only by laborious examination of the ancient texts. To that task Tischendorf gave himself entirely: "I am confronted with a sacred task," he wrote to his fiancée, "the struggle to regain the original form of the New Testament."

Despite the ancient world being infested with thieves and robbers, making travel no less perilous than in America's "wild west," Tischendorf was dedicated to his mission. Now, perched in the camel's saddle, he thought about those who had secured a number of valuable manuscripts from the monasteries, and his hopes ran high. 'One man's trash was another man's treasure' was a cliché repeated numerous times in the Near East of the nineteenth century. Tons of biblical and extrabiblical materials were stored in the monastic libraries that had sprung up in the fifth, sixth, and succeeding centuries.

Many of the monasteries survived the centuries—implanted points of refuge for the pious, dotting the biblical world. Many others succumbed to the centuries—victims of roving bands of thieves, the armies of Islam, and in a

161

few cases, to the Crusaders—the very ones who should have defended them.

St. Catherine's, Tischendorf's destination, was one of the survivors.

Tischendorf heard the signal from the caravan leader—it was time to stop for the evening. For eleven days the small train had followed the same procedure—riding from dawn until 10 A.M. and then again from 5 P.M. until nearly midnight. He felt his body shiver with pain as he slid off the camel. He walked slowly around the small rocky outcropping where they had stopped, trying to drive the numbness and stiffness from his legs.

As he lay down his aching body on his pallet, he heard himself groan in relief. Lying there, he reveled in the coolness that settled over the surface of the earth. Tischendorf pulled a blanket over himself and marveled at the incredible quietness of the desert. *I hope we'll be there by tomorrow,* he thought. They had been traversing higher ground all day and that was an indication that they were nearing the point of the Arabian peninsula and their ultimate destination—the famous monastery of St. Catherine's. *Will I be successful?* The dull pain in his body heightened his anxiety about the trip—he certainly would never be able to make another.

His two previous trips came back to him clearly as he lay under the sparkling panoply of stars.

He had been disappointed at first upon his initial arrival at St. Catherine's; not only about the condition of monastic life, but also about the library—it was ill-kept, there were only a few interesting manuscripts, and none of the New Testament. Just before he was to leave, however, he had noticed a large pile of book scraps of all kinds. "Just rubbish," Cyril the librarian explained. "Lately we have thrown two such piles into the fire so as to get them out of our way." Tischendorf made a quick inspection of the "rubbish" and noticed some of the larger pages had Greek writing on them. A quick examination revealed that it was an ancient copy of the Old Testament.

Tischendorf requested permission to take the manuscript back to Europe for study. The abbot granted him forty-three pages, but kept the remaining eighty-six. The scholar urged the monks to take good care of the remaining portion and then hurried back to Leipzig. Scrutinizing his find, he determined that the manuscript was written in the fourth century, making it a hundred years older than the Alexandrinus manuscript, which was the oldest manuscript known at that time.

It was nine years later, in 1853, before Tischendorf was able to return to St. Catherine's, but this time his trip was destined to be a failure. The monks couldn't find the eighty-six pages. Cyril, the librarian, did not know what had happened to the pages, nor did anyone else. The frustrated scholar, sure the monks were telling the truth, conducted an exhaustive search, but to no avail. His only reward for the long journey was a tiny scrap of the twenty-third chapter of Genesis, which was being used as a bookmark in a volume of short biographies of the saints.

Now, fifteen years after his initial visit,

Tischendorf was returning. *This will be my last chance,* he thought as he fell asleep.

The next morning, while the sun was casting shadows behind them, the camels skirted around a steep outcropping, then clambered almost gracefully up a slope where the lead driver halted the train. Pointing across the valley before them, his few remaining teeth glistened in the morning sun as he smiled in satisfaction. There it was—Mt. Sinai—the mountain where God spoke to Moses and where the Israelites rebelled against God. And on the face of the mountain was St. Catherine's—aloof from the vicissitudes of daily life, a granite bastion, fashioned from the fabric of the mountain and set like a rough jewel against its side.

Built like a small fortress, the monastery had endured the centuries for several reasons: high walls protected the monks, and there was no gate. Access could be gained from the valley floor only by a windlass-operated basket, dropped from an opening thirty-five feet above the ground. And in a concession to the realities of the times, a small tower had been added in the shape of a minaret to make any passing Moslems think the monastery was a mosque.

In a short time the camel train made its way below the imposing structure. A small rope with a basket attached dropped from the opening. Tischendorf knew the system well. He placed his papers in the basket, gave it a tug, and the bundle was hoisted up to the anonymous monks above. Tischendorf knew his papers would be well-received by the monks; for the first time he was making his journey under the auspices of the Russian czar, who was looked upon as the protector of the Eastern Orthodox Christians. The scholar was sure he would be received even more enthusiastically because of his credentials.

In just a moment a different rope dropped, a heavier cord than the other, and with a sturdy crossbar for the support of a man's weight. He wrapped his legs around the bar, and spinning slowly, he was hoisted up into the spiritual sanctuary.

"Professor Tischendorf!" a voice exclaimed as he stepped onto solid footing. It was the steward of the monastery.

"Brother Andrios!" Tischendorf shouted in genuine delight, for the slender man with the trim white hair had become a genuine friend during the previous visit.

"How good to see you," Tischendorf said, after the men had embraced.

"And you too, my brother," the monk replied. "The years have treated you well."

"Please, Brother Andrios. I respect you for your honesty. Please don't throw away your credibility with your flattery. I have never felt my age more acutely than in the last twelve days. I assure you, my brother, this worn-out old body will take only one more trip on the back of a camel—and that will be my return trip to Cairo."

"Please do not speak of leaving just when you have arrived, my brother. I am looking forward to your days here. We will spend many hours together, talking of many things as before. Bring up his luggage," Andrios instructed the monks working the windlass.

"Deacon Andrios," the professor lowered his voice. "I too, look forward to talking with you, but as you can understand, I have one subject of conversation which is primary—not a day has gone by in the last nine years that I have not thought about it: Have the missing pages been discovered?"

The monk looked directly into the eyes of the professor, his countenance betraying the bad news he was about to share. "My friend, I am sorry to disappoint you. I think I know something of spending one's life in a singular pursuit—each of us in his own is trying to serve God . . . but I am sorry, the manuscript pages have never been found."

The professor had prepared himself for this response, or at least he thought he had. He had told himself repeatedly that the manuscript would not have turned up. Yet in the corners of his mind, in areas he steadfastly refused to nourish or even acknowledge, a faint hope had grown, like a stunted plant hidden from the sun. A wave of pain swept through the scholar, and his body trembled slightly. He had not realized how stubborn the unacknowledged and unnourished hope had been.

The monk saw the color pass from the scholar's rigid face. "But we will look," he said in an encouraging tone. "We will look."

Tischendorf swallowed with difficulty. "Yes," he said, "we certainly will look."

"Come, my friend, let me show you to your quarters. I will make sure that you are undisturbed for the rest of the afternoon. And when you are rested we will share our evening meal together and then make plans for our search for the manuscript."

Tischendorf had thought that he would want to begin the search for the missing eighty-six pages immediately upon his arrival, but he realized the wisdom of the monk's advice. He suddenly felt very tired.

"Yorghos, please come here." The priest summoned a round-faced young man with a bored expression who sat on the pile of Tischendorf's baggage across the room. He, like all the other monks, wore a black robe, a simple high-crowned hat, and his hair tied behind in a neat bun. "I am assigning Yorghos, one of our newest members, to assist you while you are here."

"Thank you Deacon Andrios, but I don't think it will be nec-. . . ."

"Please," the monk interrupted, "if you don't mind, I would appreciate it if you would keep the young man occupied." He leaned closer to the scholar's ear. "Frankly, I need something for him to do. I have given him numerous jobs and he has shown no ability in any area. Prehaps he can demonstrate hospitality—he certainly can't work in the garden or clean the grounds."

"You called for me, sir?" There was no insolence in the overweight young man's voice, just a sense of detached weariness.

"Professor Tischendorf is a world-renowned scholar and a good friend. Please show him to the guest room and see to it that every effort is made to insure his comfort during his stay here. If you will excuse me, my good friend, I will see to it that your drivers and camels are attended to. I look forward to breaking bread with you this evening."

Yorghos placed the baggage in the tidy little guest room and started to leave when the professor asked him, "How long have you been here, Yorghos?"

"Four months. But it seems much longer than that."

"Are you not happy here?"

"There are too many rules," the puffy-faced young monk-to-be answered.

"Certainly you must have known the nature of the rules of the order before you came. If they were too restrictive, why did you come?"

"I didn't. Or at least I didn't come willingly. My father sent me. He's a merchant back in Athens. He was determined that one of his sons would be a priest or a monk. I was the youngest and neither of my two brothers took vows, so my father sent me here."

"How old are you, Yorghos?"

"Nineteen, nearly twenty."

"And you do not like monastic life?"

There was an unintelligible grunt from the young man.

"Pardon me?" the professor asked.

"Oh, it wouldn't be so bad with a few changes."

"And what changes would you make, my young friend?"

Yorghos looked at the professor carefully. He seemed hesitant to answer, but after scrutinizing the older man, he must have decided that he meant no harm. "The food," he mumbled.

"Pardon me?"

"The food. I would change the food. I have nothing against serving God—I just don't see why we have to do it on an empty stomach. I will starve to death if I stay here much longer!"

Tischendorf could hardly keep from smiling as he looked at the corpulent figure of the young man—there was little chance that starvation was imminent.

"How is one supposed to pray when his stomach growls like a wild bear?"

Tischendorf noticed the young man was looking at the luggage. "Oh, excuse me," the professor asked, "could I offer you something? I'm afraid there's not much. . . ."

"Any cheese?" Yorghos asked as he began sorting through the professor's sack.

"No, I'm afraid the only thing left is a few dates—it's been several days since we were able to stock any supplies."

"This *is* a godforsaken area, isn't it? Can't get a decent piece of cheese! One goat could eat in one day all the grass you can see from the top of the mountain. And if there *was* a goat around, who would have the patience to wait for cheese? Woe to the goat that Yorghos discovered—his throat would be slit and his carcass roasting over a fire before he knew what happened to him!"

Tischendorf smiled at the comic figure before him, down on his knees rummaging through the food sack.

"But I fear," Yorghos continued, "that these poor teeth will never chew a piece of meat again. Back home in Athens my mother would prepare a great rack of lamb brushed with vinegar and a light touch of garlic. And there would be great heaps of fresh bread, and bowls of fruit, and. . . ." Yorghos caught himself. "But never again."

"So you expect to remain here at St. Catherine's?"

The comic-tragic figure looked at the professor balefully. "Have you ever visited the ossuary, professor?"

Tischendorf was familiar with the burial chamber on the monastery's grounds where hundreds and hundreds of skulls lay in gruesome, heaping mounds, the last remains of those who, through the centuries, had chosen to live and die within those walls. "Yes, I have," the professor answered.

"Before long, poor Yorghos' head will be numbered among that pile—the victim of starvation."

Tischendorf coughed to cover his laughter. There was no doubt that there were several dozen pounds between him and starvation, but the absolute seriousness with which Yorghos considered his plight caused the professor to have to stifle his laughter.

"Professor, are you all right? This is an evil climate. I hope you have not contracted some dread disease."

"Oh no, I'm sure it's nothing serious," the professor said as he wiped his watering eyes with a cloth. "I'm sure I will be fine after I've rested."

Yorghos put two more dates in his mouth, and, having decided it would be impolite to stay longer, put the remaining half-dozen in the lining of his cloak. He dismissed himself with an unpracticed bow, wiping his sticky hands on his cloak.

"I hope we will talk again," the professor said.

"Yes, of course, sir."

Tischendorf smiled as he closed the door behind the boy. There had been weeks of anxious preparation for the trip and then twelve tortuous, tedious days on the camel, so he was grateful for the relief from the pent-up tension the portly servant had offered. The search for the manuscript had robbed him of the most basic joys. *Ah, the manuscript.* For a few minutes he had forgotten it. He lay on the simple bed and felt the aches in his body drain away. He slept the sleep of one who had spent eleven consecutive nights on the rocky desert ground.

Professor Tischendorf was awakened by a gentle rapping at the door. He had considerable difficulty orienting himself. He saw the shaft of light through the window—it was practically parallel with the floor—and he determined that he must have been asleep for nearly three hours.

"Sir." The voice at the door was Yorghos.

"Coming, Yorghos."

The professor opened the door. "Sir, Deacon Andrios has asked me to summon you for the evening meal. It will be served in thirty minutes. I have brought you a basin of water and a towel."

"Thank you, Yorghos. Excuse my dazed appearance. I don't think I realized the extent of my fatigue. As the saying goes, I slept like a baby."

Yorghos, looking as if he were unaccustomed to small talk, smiled weakly, but said nothing.

"Well," the professor said. "Again, I thank you for the water and I shall be prompt for dinner."

Yorghos dismissed himself with another awkward bow and the professor set about preparing himself for dinner.

Several minutes later Deacon Andrios came by to escort Tischendorf to the dining hall. About three dozen monks sat at the long tables, the length of their service told in their beards—some jet-black, others peppered, and a few, like a proof of the purity they sought to attain, fell from their faces in a cascade of creamy white.

The meal was simple, befitting those who sought simplicity: a thin soup, yogurt, fresh bread, and a vegetable Tischendorf did not recognize. He saw Yorghos across the room, seated in a special area for novitiates. Yorghos caught the professor's eyes and wrinkled up his nose in noiseless commentary of the evening's fare.

"Deacon Andrios, would it be possible to visit the library after dinner?"

"I had planned to invite you," Andrios responded. "I think you will be impressed at the changes we have made. We owe much to you for the improvements. Our new librarian, Demetrios, who succeeded Cyril upon his death some years ago, has done an outstanding job. Soon after he assumed his new duty I showed him the letter you sent after your departure—the one in which you recommended cataloguing all the volumes in the library.

Demetrios was thrilled with the project and did, I feel, a very good job."

"But the eighty-six pages—they did not turn up?"

"No," the monk lowered his head. "I'm sorry, my brother. I do not know what became of those pages. I think I know something of what they mean to you and I will do everything possible to help you."

"Andrios, my friend, I appreciate your concern. We are somewhat alike, are we not? We both desire to serve God—you in a life of prayer and devotion, and me, my goal has always been to bring God's Word to His people—and there is nothing that would aid me more in my lifelong quest than to secure those eighty-six pages—pages I once held in my hands here within these walls!"

When the two men were finished with their meal they made their way toward the library. Although the exterior of the monastery was austere, the interior, especially the rooms of worship, were a kaleidoscope of form and color. Rich rugs lay on tesselated floors; ornate candelabras ornamented with painted ostrich eggs hung above; a brocade-decked altar held metal-bound lectionaries; brass candlesticks, taller than the monks, were set at the door like sentries; and on the walls hung some of the greatest treasures of Byzantine art, hundreds of colorful icons.

Tischendorf stepped onto the marble floors of the nave of the church. Reflections of red vigil lights glittered on the marble slabs. High above him in the arching half-dome was a majestic scene—a mosaic of the transfiguration of Christ—a triumph of early Byzantine art.

As the pair moved down the corridor to the library, a smile came across Tischendorf's face as he asked: "Tell me, Andrios—your novitiate, Yorghos—do you think he is temperamentally suited to life here at St. Catherine's?"

"Ah, Yorghos," Andrios answered, his amusement evident. "A likeable young fellow, but as you phrased it, there is some genuine concern over the 'suitability of his temperament.' "

"What will happen with him? Will he remain?"

"No. Yorghos no doubt will see the lilacs come to bloom on the Athenian hills this summer—and consume all the meat and cheese he desires, I might add. But he knows nothing of this. I have a stack of letters from his mother—he has seen none of them—crying over her 'baby.' It seems Yorghos' father sent him here in a fit of anger. We occasionally have young men like Yorghos come here, some even by their own volition, perhaps in a surge of religious piety; but when the time comes for final vows, our austere life serves as a crucible to separate those who are genuinely suited for monastic life from those who are not."

In answer to their knock, the library door was opened by a slight man in his late twenties. "Professor Tischendorf," he said enthusiastically, "I have heard so much about you and your work! I am Demetrios. Please come in."

Tischendorf noticed immediately the change in the room. Upon his initial visit he had found the library a jungle of scattered manuscripts, laying in dirty stacks, generally ignored and unused for centuries. Demetrios had done his job well—the yellowed, aging manuscripts lay in organized fashion on shelves lining the room. The Greek manuscripts were predominant, but there was a section of Coptic, Latin, Syriac, and Aramaic manuscripts.

"You have done good work, Demetrios—and valuable work. Scholars of the next centuries will profit from what you have done."

The young monk, beaming from the commendation of the eminent scholar, bowed graciously.

The professor slid his hands along a few of the shelved books. "The eighty six pages—I'm sure you know what I'm speaking of—there was no hint of those pages when you catalogued these volumes?"

"No, professor, I'm sorry," the young man replied. "Of course I have not been through every page of every volume. . . ." He gestured around the room in suggestion of the immensity of such a task.

"Perhaps we can't examine every page," the professor responded as he turned to Andrios, "but if I had four or five men, I think we could adequately cover every volume in eight or ten days."

"That could be arranged," Andrios replied.

"Could we begin tomorrow?"

"Certainly," Andrios said, and Demetrios nodded in agreement.

Tischendorf was awakened by a loud noise. Dull, rhythmic, and insistent, the sound of metal on metal punctuated the darkness. He reached for the pocket watch by his bed. It was 3:30 A.M. The sound was that of the

175

*semandron*, a metal bar beaten by a hammer, the summons for the monks to assemble for the first liturgy of the day.

Tischendorf lay awake on his bed for several minutes, then slipped on his clothes and made his way to a small balcony overlooking the nave of the church. There, already assembled, was the population of the monastery, kneeling and chanting. The multitude of candles gave an eerie and unearthly glow to the room as the monks joined in devoting the first three hours of the day to God. The eerie other-worldness of the scene was lightened somewhat when Tischendorf noticed Yorghos, kneeling at the outer edge of the assembly, prayer book in hand. The young novitiate's head kept drooping to one side as he dozed off; then he would snap it back into position with a start.

Tischendorf smiled at the unlikely monk, watched the liturgical drama for a few more moments, then slipped back to his room and slept till dawn.

After breakfast Tischendorf met with the small group of monks Andrios had selected to help him with his task. He outlined the responsibilities and tried to impart to them the significance of the search. The men accepted the work eagerly and as the work was divided, they diligently began. Tischendorf himself would be responsible for the sheaves of unbound works, for he thought that would be the most likely place for the missing sheets of Scripture.

The days slid by in unchanging precision— four, five, six days of unfruitful search for the eighty-six pages. "I don't understand it,"

Tischendorf said to his host, Andrios, his voice tinged with despair. "Where could those sheets be? I have personally examined all the unbound sheaves in the library and in one or two more days we will have covered every volume—and still no signs of the missing pages!"

"I share your frustration, my friend," Andrios replied. "I'm afraid you again have made this long journey for no purpose."

"Perhaps not. Let's not lose hope," the professor replied, but he did not talk like a man who harbored a great deal of hope.

That evening, as usual, Tischendorf shared his meal with Andrios.

"My brother," Andrios began, "I have been summoned to Cairo. I leave tomorrow to spend a month with the abbot."

"I'm sorry to hear that, Andrios," the professor responded, obviously disenchanted by the news. "I wish we could make the trip together—the journey would be more bearable—are you sure you must leave tomorrow? In a few more days. . . ."

"Yes, my friend," Andrios interrupted. "I must leave tomorrow. I too had hoped that we could make the journey together. I thought perhaps your search would have been rewarded at this point and we could depart together. But I have known for weeks before your arrival that I would have to depart on this date."

"But what if. . . ."

"Excuse me for interrupting you, but I think I have predicted your question. Here, take this." He gave the professor a small slip of paper. On it was written:

*Dr. Constantine Tischendorf has my permission, at his discretion, to remove any manuscripts found in the library and transport them to me in Cairo.*

*Deacon Andrios of St. Catherine's*
*January 31, 1859*

"But who will be in charge in your absence?"

"Deacon Vasilis."

"Vasilis?" Tischendorf said. "Not *him!* You know he has opposed my research since the beginning. You have told me so yourself. He voted against allowing me to study the forty-three pages on my first trip here."

"What you say is true. I cannot deny it. Vasilis seems distrustful of all outsiders. I would prefer to think our lives and our ministry have been enriched by those like yourself, who have visited us; but Vasilis, for reasons I do not know, would prefer we close our doors to the outside world entirely. But I have no choice in this matter, he is Keeper of the Plate, and as such, his office makes him the responsible party in my absence."

"But. . . ."

"Please, my brother, there is no other choice," Andrios said firmly.

Before Tischendorf could protest further, he realized that Vasilis was standing beside him, his thin lips composed in a collusive smile on his yellow hatchet face.

"Deacon Vasilis," Andrios said, "I have informed Professor Tischendorf of my departure. Please be certain he is granted every consideration during my absence."

The monk bowed slightly in acknowledgment, but Tischendorf noticed the expression

178

on his pallid face remained unchanged.

"Brother Tischendorf," Andrios said, as Vasilis slipped away, "I trust you will call on me in Cairo."

Tischendorf, still watching Vasilis, did not respond. "Pardon me, Andrios. What did you say?"

"When you come to Cairo," Andrios repeated, "I hope you will contact me."

"Oh, yes, certainly Andrios."

After the meal the two men walked down the corridors to Tischendorf's room. Andrios continued to try to reassure the scholar that Vasilis would cause him no problem and Tischendorf was partially consoled; but the next morning his concern was heightened. He and the handful of monks were going about their research in the library when Vasilis appeared. Without a word, hands folded in a pious, perverted way, he made a circuit of the room, pausing to look over the shoulder of each of the monks sitting at the table, as if to insure that nothing was out of order.

Two days later the monks completed their audit of the library and no hint of the elusive eighty-six pages was discovered. Tischendorf, with Deacon Andrios' prior approval, began a thorough search of the monastery—every room, niche, and closet was examined. The entire population of the order was briefed, and they joined in the search—but to no avail. No trace of the missing manuscript was uncovered.

On February 5, 1859, the frustrated scholar gave up his quest. He sent orders to the camel drivers to be ready for departure on February seventh. On his final day in the Sinai,

Tischendorf climbed the Mountain of Moses and sat at its peak surveying the scene around him. Great ridges of charcoal and rose-colored ridges rose up to the horizon. Like tumultuous waves frozen in time the granite peaks heaved up toward the sky. For several hours the disconsolate scholar sat ensconced in the rocks. Finally, as dusk suffused the valley, he slipped out of his rocky retreat back to the monastery.

Yorghos brought some hot tea to the scholar's room and was about to excuse himself. "Please Yorghos," the professor said, "have a seat for a few minutes."

Yorghos politely took a stool in the corner as the professor began assembling his belongings in his suitcase. "You know I leave tomorrow?"

Yorghos assented with a nod.

Tischendorf poured himself a cup of the tea and offered some to Yorghos, who declined. "Perhaps the trip was not a total waste. . ." Tischendorf said, speaking as if he were talking to a colleague. "Perhaps the extensive cataloguing we did will prove valuable to the next generation of scholars. No doubt there are many valuable works in the library, and I should not discount their value simply because of my failure to find those elusive eighty-six pages. . . . But I had hoped . . . yes, I admit it—I had hoped to find the missing manuscript. I tried *not* to hope, but it was as futile as trying to will my heart not to beat—it was possessed of an energy and volition of its own and I could not suppress it.

"Yes, Yorghos," the professor went on, looking out the small window, "I had hoped, but I have failed."

180

"I know where some manuscripts are," Yorghos said quietly.

A mild breeze blew in off the desert and the candles waved and flickered. The professor turned around deliberately and placed his teacup on the table.

"Pardon me?" the professor said.

Yorghos looked around timidly as if someone might overhear.

"I know where some manuscripts are," he repeated.

The professor sat on the edge of the bed directly facing the young novitiate, his intelligent eyes flashing all over the young man, trying to make some sense of this new information. "Please . . . tell me of these manuscripts."

Yorghos lowered his voice. "One night soon after I came here, I was hungry . . . and I thought perhaps I could find something to eat. I didn't know my way around very well so I ended up in a strange room above Deacon Vasilis' office—a lot of old furniture was stored in there. I thought perhaps I might find some stores put away, but I was not so lucky."

Yorghos paused for a moment and looked at the door. "I hope I will not get in trouble for. . . ."

"Please," the professor interrupted, "your secret is safe with me. Please go on."

"While I was going through the furniture, I noticed a stack of old papers. I did not pay attention to them—the library is full of old papers, and I was mainly looking for some food."

"These 'papers' you saw—was the inscription on them Greek?"

"Yes, I think so."

"And did they appear to be very old?"

"I suppose so."

Tischendorf, his mind whirling, tried to assess the situation. If he asked Vasilis for permission to search the room, he would very likely be turned down. Or at least Vasilis might put him off until Andrios returned. A delay would be as bad as a denial—the camels would be ready to depart at dawn. *If only Andrios were here!*

"Yorghos, take me to the papers you saw."

"Now?" Yorghos asked incredulously.

"Yes, now. We have no time to waste." Tischendorf took Yorghos by the arm and escorted him down the corridors. The melodic chants of the monks, engaged in the evening services, reverberated down the hallways.

When they reached the room, Tischendorf tested the door. "It's locked."

"Of course, sir," Yorghos replied. "It's always locked."

"Well, how did you get in?"

Yorghos pointed sheepishly above him. There was a small window about twelve feet above them.

"How did you get in there?"

"I stacked some tables on top of each other."

"You must have been very hungry. Quickly, where are the tables?"

Yorghos brought two small tables from down the corridor. The professor steadied them and nodded to Yorghos to climb. The young novitiate stalled for a moment, incredulous that the eminent professor was an accomplice to this adventure.

"Quickly, Yorghos—before the services end!"

Yorghos climbed atop the two tables and with great difficulty pulled himself into the opening. For a moment he teetered in the window and it was not certain whether the young man would fall in or out, but finally he slid unceremoniously into the storage room.

"Are you all right?" the professor asked in a whisper.

"Yes," came the reply, as Yorghos poked his head out the vent. "I need a candle."

The professor climbed atop the tables and placed a candle in Yorghos' outstretched hand. "Please hurry." Yorghos nodded and then disappeared into the room. He went to the corner where he thought he had seen the stack of manuscripts. He unstacked some anti-quated furniture. Dust filled the air and he sneezed uncontrollably two, three, four times. In the hallway, Tischendorf cringed at the noise. He looked down the corridor, but no one was visible. He could still hear the sounds emanating from the evening service.

In the storeroom, Yorghos composed himself, wiping his nose vigorously. He removed some additional pieces of furniture and then he saw them—four stacks of loose sheets of papyrus bound in red cloth, plus an ornate wooden scroll. Outside, he heard the professor's voice, "Yorghos, the chanting has stopped. Please hurry!"

Yorghos stacked the manuscripts on top of each other and placed the scroll on top of the heap. He stumbled through the disheveled room, but as he positioned himself to climb out the window the cylindrical scroll rolled out of his arms and onto the floor.

Yorghos took the candle to look for the scroll. Spotting it under a discarded desk, he spread himself facedown on the floor to try to reach it. With great effort he extended his stubby arms to the point that his fingers were on the scroll. As he tried to grasp it, however, it rolled further away.

"Yorghos!"

Yorghos scrambled up from the floor, reached the stacks out to the waiting arms of the professor and scurried out himself. Quickly they replaced the tables and made their way back to the guest room just as the monks dismissed their assembly.

Inside the room, Yorghos brushed the dust from his cloak. Tischendorf, gasping, said "God forgive me if I have sinned."

Catching his breath he placed the papyrus stacks on his bed and began untying the knots. At first glance he knew he had found his prize! There was the same handwriting he had learned to know fifteen years before. Tischendorf wanted to scream with delight! But what was this? There were more than 86 pages—in fact, he discovered an additional 112 pages of the Old Testament! That was incredible enough, but as the aging scholar opened the *second* stack, to his utter amazement he found the entire New Testament in the same hand! The two smaller stacks yielded two extrabiblical works, the *Epistle of Barnabas* and the *Shepherd of Hermas*, both known previously only by title.

Tischendorf knelt before the bed, eyes flashing over the remarkable treasure spread out before him. He ran over to Yorghos, hugged

184

and kissed him, and danced him around the room. Yorghos, who could not understand why anyone would be excited about a pile of musty old papers, thought the scholar had lost his mind. "Thank you, Yorghos. Thank you, Yorghos," the professor kept repeating, and then he fairly jumped back to the bed and his treasure.

Lost in a bliss Yorghos could not comprehend, the professor took out his notebook and began jotting down notes as he read the stack of papers. Yorghos dismissed himself. "I will see you in the morning as you depart professor."

"Uh, yes," the professor mumbled without looking up, engrossed in the ancient works. "Yes, in the morning."

The next morning the professor's eyes were bleary and red as he said good-bye to Yorghos and Demetrios, for he had stayed awake all night reading the manuscripts; but there was more than a hint of energy in those eyes as he said his final farewells to the men.

In a few moments he and his precious manuscripts were aboard the awaiting camel and he waved as the camel train moved out of sight.

Only at that moment, as the professor went out of sight, did Yorghos remember. *The scroll.* In a rare moment of lucid thought, he realized he should get the scroll to the professor. He ran clumsily down the corridor until he came to Deacon Vasilis's room. The door was unlocked. He peeped in. The room was empty; the deacon must have stepped out momentarily. Quickly Yorghos ran up the stairs. Lying prostrate on the floor, he was able to grasp the wooden cylinder. Pushing it in his robe, he darted out of the room to the monastery's exit. Enlisting the help of one of the monks, he had himself lowered to the ground below where he quickly saddled a donkey.

Yorghos made a resolute effort to overtake Tischendorf's train, but his stubborn beast, no doubt troubled by the ponderous burden he was bearing, did not share his master's exuberance.

"Go, you four-legged son of Satan," Yorghos goaded the animal, but to no avail. He cajoled and threatened the donkey unmercifully, but the animal kept its pace.

After little more than an hour's ride, Yorghos was sure he was making no headway on the camel train. Stopping as he came around a spur overlooking a level plain, he tried to see the professor's caravan, but there was no trace of it. He decided to turn back, but at that moment his nose detected an aroma he had not known in several months— roasted meat! While inhaling great quantities of desert air to verify his first impression, he noticed a couple of brightly colored tents set in the rocks just below him; and a thin trail of smoke wafted up into the dry desert air.

A few minutes later Yorghos sat cross-legged near the fire, chewing voraciously on the last few morsels of meat on a bone. Two dark-eyed children giggled at the strange young man as he added the bone to the pile beside him. It was only a scrawny goat, the victim of a predator in the night, but the children's father, seated near Yorghos, had heard the animal's pitiful screams, and although he had not been able to save the goat, he was at least able to intervene soon enough to rob the predator of his kill—a most fortuitous circumstance for Yorghos, who continued to gnaw on the roasted goat.

When the last stringy morsel of the goat had been consumed, Yorghos belched loudly several times, and then realized he should get back to the monastery. The Bedouin smiled broadly as Yorghos tried to show his gratitude without the benefit of a common language. The gratitude was obvious and well-received by the hospitable Bedouin, but suddenly it occurred to Yorghos that he had nothing to offer in gratitude. What could he do? As he pondered his dilemma, he felt the weight of the scroll in the pouch next to his hip. *Should he offer the scroll as a gift? He couldn't catch up with the professor, that was obvious. And it certainly was doing no one any good at the monastery—no one seemed to know that it existed.*

Yorghos slid his hand into his cloak and withdrew the ornate cylinder. Graciously, he offered it to the Bedouin, who obviously had no idea of the object's function. Nevertheless, he seemed to appreciate the rich carving and accepted the gift, showing it to his wife, who smiled her approval as well.

Yorghos again thanked his host for the meal, and feeling slightly nauseous, thought it best that he walk back to the monastery. So, leading the donkey, he began his trek. As he disappeared over the hill, the Bedouin waved, holding the scroll in his other hand.

All of the stacks of paper on the chief of
police's desk—and there were several—were
held in place by paperweights. An oscillating
Japanese fan swept back and forth across the
room, creating a wave of ripples among the
profusion of papers. The chief himself, a
medium-sized man with a thick black mus-
tache, sat behind the desk and listened attentively to the professor and Samuel as they
explained the situation. Jim and Sarah sat to
one side.

"The man you describe," the chief
answered, "sounds like one of a group of men
we've been watching for some time. They
moved into one of the new housing projects
outside of town just a few weeks ago—they
appear suspicious, if you know what I mean—
but we don't have any specific charges against
them. Perhaps it would be a good idea if we
drove out there to take a look."

A few minutes later they had parked the car a few hundred yards from the housing project, a concrete and stucco series of buildings. Not a shrub or tree softened its dry harshness against the landscape. A group of women sat in the building's shade. A few small children played in the dusty rubble, while workmen were unloading blocks for another building.

Jim mounted his longest telephoto lens on his camera and focused it on the building. He could see some activity through the curtainless windows. "Kavakis, see if you can determine if your ex-digger is inside."

Kavakis took the camera and began scrutinizing the men inside. "I believe that's our man," he said.

"Do you see the scroll?" the professor asked.

"No, but let me look again." He surveyed the room through the open window. "Oh no," he said flatly.

"What is it?" the professor asked, his face showing his agony. "Is it the scroll?"

"No, I don't see the scroll," Kavakis answered. "Here, Jim, take a look—the window to the right, in the corner."

Jim took the camera. He could see a small stack of what appeared to be boxes of some sort covered by a sheet. "All I see is . . ." he started, but he stopped abruptly. "Oh, now I see what you're talking about." In the lower corner of the stack, where the sheet did not reach to the floor, Jim saw some familiar stenciled letters: "U.S. ARMY EXPLOSIVES."

Jim turned to the group. "Dynamite. Looks like enough to blow the building to smithereens."

190

As each member of the group assessed this new complication, the police officer spoke: "Last week there was dynamite stolen not far from here. A joint American-Israeli group was building a command post. The guard dogs were poisoned and a few cases of dynamite were taken." He thought for a moment, and then added, "I'm afraid this will mean that I must contact the army."

"But what about the scroll?" the professor pleaded. "For every minute we delay, the chances something could go wrong are increased."

"I understand your feelings, Dr. Crawford, but look down there—a lot of innocent people are in great danger. My first priority is to protect them."

As they drove back to town, the police chief spoke again: "I don't think it's professional terrorists we're dealing with. More than likely this is just a pack of common thieves—stealing whatever they can and selling it for whatever price they can get. No doubt, however, those explosives would have ended up in the hands of terrorists if we had not discovered them."

"Do you think the army will . . ." the professor began.

"Will they try to recover the scroll?" the chief interrupted. "You of all people, Professor, should realize that we are a nation of archaeologists. We all have a stake in our history—it is what binds us together. I will make sure that the commander knows there is a valuable artifact inside the building. I am sure he will do everything possible to secure it safely."

That evening as darkness approached, Dr.

Crawford, Samuel, Sarah, and Jim were back at their vantage point near the housing project. The police chief, along with a few of his men, was with them. On another road, well-hidden, was an Israeli unit of soldiers.

"The plan is simple," the chief explained. "As soon as it's dark, the soldiers will quickly begin evacuating all of the people. Hopefully it can be done quietly enough to avoid arousing any suspicion. Then the building will be surrounded and the thieves will be asked to surrender. Hopefully it will go smoothly."

As he spoke, they could see the first soldiers begin approaching the apartments farthest from the explosives. Gradually the inhabitants began filtering out into the nearby hills. Jim kept a watchful eye on the suspects.

"Can you see anything, Jim?" the professor asked.

"Everything seems normal inside the building."

The soldiers had evacuated all the buildings except the one closest to the potential danger. As a soldier alerted the family, Jim noticed some activity in the building he was watching.

"Someone's stirring inside," he said, still watching through the telephoto lens. "The front door is opening. I can't see him now that he's out of the light!"

At that moment the figure standing at the front door struck a match to light a cigarette.

"He's stepped outside for a smoke," Jim said. "Maybe he won't notice anything."

But Jim was wrong. The man turned to see the Israeli soldier shepherding the family next door to safety.

In a second the man jumped back inside.

"The lights are off," Jim said. "I think they're on to us."

A metallic voice came over a speaker. "This is Colonel Yigal of the Israeli army. Come out quickly and surrender."

"Oh no!" Jim said, still looking through the lens.

"What is it, Jim?" Kavakis asked.

"A fire! There's a fire inside!"

Samuel, Sarah, and Dr. Crawford looked for themselves—the flame was visible to their unaided eyes. Instinctively Jim stood up and took a step toward the building.

The voice from somewhere behind started again: "This is. . . ."

The entire summer night blew up in their faces. The first explosion was followed by an even greater one, and the landscape was washed out in the brilliant light. Jim turned back toward the professor—his face, illuminated by a series of smaller explosions, was wrenched in pain.

Jim was angry. *Isn't this the way it always ends up? There are always a few well-intentioned people trying to do something constructive, but their plans are thwarted by someone with guns or knives or dynamite.*

He cursed under his breath.

The next morning Jim found Dr. Crawford at his customary place in the dining area.

"You don't give up, do you?" Jim said, nodding at the open Bible.

"What do you mean, Jim?"

"What I mean is, it seems to me like God's side always loses. I couldn't sleep last night for thinking about that stupid scroll! It doesn't

193

mean anything to me in particular, but I know it was important to you—and it got blown to smithereens! Here you are, along with Sarah and Samuel, trying to accomplish something constructive, something that might be of help to the human race, and it's gone in a puff of smoke. I've been all over the world. It's always the same story—stupidity and greed win out over everything else. It would seem like you would give up."

"Jim," the professor began slowly, "I must confess I didn't sleep that well myself. Thinking about a manuscript that had survived nearly twenty centuries . . . and to have it destroyed before my very eyes—it seemed too ironic, too cruel. But I have been reading some words by someone who was familiar with this land; he traversed it and ruled it some three thousand years ago.

*How long, O Lord? Wilt Thou forget me forever?*
*How long wilt Thou hide Thy face from me?*
*How long shall I take counsel in my soul,*
*Having sorrow in my heart all the day?*
*How long will my enemy be exalted over me?*

*Consider and answer me, O Lord, my God;*
*Enlighten my eyes, lest I sleep the sleep of death,*
*Lest my enemy say, "I have overcome him,"*
*Lest my adversaries rejoice when I am shaken.*

*But I have trusted in Thy lovingkindness;*
*My heart shall rejoice in Thy salvation.*
*I will sing to the Lord,*
*Because He has dealt bountifully with me.*[1]

[1]Psalm 13.

194

"Notice how many times David asks the question, 'How long?' Nothing could describe my emotions better than that right now. Perhaps we modern men have changed much less than we think. David knew everything we know of frustration and alienation, and his spirit responded as ours—'How long, Lord?'

"But I find some consolation in David's response to his vexations. In the last part of this psalm he says, 'I will sing to the Lord because He has dealt bountifully with me.' He, like the most modern of modern man standing in the flux of time, was grappling with his present circumstances, but able to face the future because of how trustworthy the Lord has been in the past. There's a song I like very much that says, among other things, 'Because He lives, I can face tomorrow.' When we grapple with the great issues of life—like the existence of evil—sometimes one could come to the point of saying, 'I can't face tomorrow.' Fortunately David overcame that temptation—not because he understood all the issues—but because he knew the nature of God and he knew God had been good to him. And I derive some consolation and encouragement from the words of this fellow-struggler. David didn't give up. Neither shall I. He faced his tomorrow. I intend to face mine. He sang unto the Lord. So shall I. But fortunately for you," he laughed, "I will not sing now. Let's make some coffee."

At the same time Dr. Crawford and Jim were preparing their morning coffee, several miles away Abdul Ibn-Taleb was cursing his donkey with a special fervor. The stubborn animal had found a juicy bush on the slope of a small wadi, and it was enjoying the delectable leaves despite the tirade of its master.

Abdul was a traveling merchant, one who had counterparts in every continent of the world, men who eked out their living by bridging the distance between those at the edge of civilization and the towns that provided the items needed for existence at those remote spots. His obstinate donkey was laden with his offerings: needles, thread, material, brightly-colored scarves, cooking utensils, knives, and dozens of other items including dry-cell batteries.

These confrontations between beast and master were not rare, and invariably ended only when the donkey had filled its belly. Abdul ordinarily would have simply sat down and waited on his animal, but the smoke rising over the hill had aroused his curiosity. *What could be burning?*

He decided to break a branch off the bush. He would have never hit the animal with it, but he thought he might threaten the animal by holding the raised limb with both hands. The donkey chewed on, in complete disregard for the ludicrous man in his face.

"I will bash in your skull and roast your scrawny carcass on a spit!"

Still the donkey continued, chewing vigorously with its big yellow teeth.

"Stupid beast! I will slice you into pieces and feed you to. . . ."

At that moment Abdul noticed something at the base of the bush. He quit his tirade momentarily, put down the limb, and reached under the bush.

"What's this?" he said as he examined the object. "Some kind of scroll." He turned the cylinder over in his hands, admiring the handwork. He looked around to be certain he wasn't being watched, and with a shrug he dropped the scroll into one of the many pouches hanging on the donkey's back.

When the animal had completed its breakfast, Abdul continued up the hill toward the smoke.

He was amazed at what he saw—a concrete-block building blown off its foundation, with supporting timbers smoldering all around. The adjacent building had caved in on the side nearest the explosion. It certainly had been an explosion, Abdul reasoned, because he could see the circular indentation in the earth that must have been the impact point.

He circulated among those who were clearing up the rubble, but everyone seemed preoccupied with the recent disaster, and since he was not able to sell even a spool of thread, he led his donkey down the road toward the south.

Early that afternoon, just as the students and workers were breaking up from their midday meal, Kavakis's Jeep came roaring into the camp. Jim was taking some additional photographs of the digging site, but he came down quickly when he saw Kavakis rush into Dr. Crawford's quarters.

"What's going on?" he asked Sarah as she came out of the building and headed toward the Jeep.

"The scroll may not have been destroyed! The police have a lead. Hop in!"

Jim clambered in as the professor and Kavakis hurried from the building. They climbed into the Jeep and Kavakis explained as he drove: "Our ex-digger was caught in the hills about daybreak. Late this morning he admitted stealing the scroll, *but*, he says he took the scroll with him when he fled."

"Where is it?" Jim asked.

"Says he threw it into the wadi as he was running away."

"Do you believe him?"

"Not necessarily—he may be trying to win our sympathy. But what choice do we have?"

At that moment the speeding Jeep met a tattered old man leading a heavily ladened donkey. As the Jeep roared by, Sarah waved in apology to the old man for stirring up so much dust. The old man muttered something to the effect of "Crazy Americans" and trudged on.

# 12

Jim stood motionless, staring out the window. The sounds of the street twenty stories below were barely audible.

Alex burst into the room. "Jim, here are the first layouts—they're great! *Look* at this! You're going to sell a lot of magazines for me, Jim."

Jim turned his head as Alex spread the layout sheets on the polished conference table, but he turned back to the window after only a glance.

"Simpson, our assistant editor, wants to talk with you again," Alex said, straightening the sheets into two neat rows. "Just wants to verify some facts and get your OK on the copy. . . . Jim, are you listening to me?"

"I hear you," Jim replied flatly.

"Hey, Jim. I know you feel bad about losing the scroll, but. . . ."

" 'But it makes a great story, any way.' Is that what you were going to say, Alex?"

"Well, not in those words, maybe. . . . Hey, Jim, sit down." Alex took Jim by the shoulders and helped seat him at the table. Giant glossy prints covered the table—the Qumran excavation, the view from Masada, the burned-out building, the apprehended criminals, two grainy black and white blow-ups of the scroll and Ahmoud and Yosuf. There were some bold letters above the lead photograph: MYSTERY OF THE MANU-SCRIPT.

"Jim, are you sure about this leave of absence thing? Why don't you just take a week off and. . . ."

"I'm sure," Jim interrupted. "Dr. Crawford has invited me to spend some time with him at the college. Sarah's going to be there, too." Jim was still interested in getting to know her better. "I don't know how long I'll be gone. 'cause I'm just going to take it one day at a time."

There was a knock at the door.

"That must be Simpson," Alex said. He answered the door and led the editor to the conference table.

"Just want to verify everything before we go to press," he said, opening a spiral notebook. "First of all, although the scroll was never recovered, Dr. Crawford has said that no real damage has been done."

"That's right," Jim replied. "He said that there is virtually no question that the Gospel of Luke as we know it today is the same as it was when Luke wrote it—sometime before A.D. 60."

"And the boy and his grandfather," Simpson went on, ". . .you were able to get their land back?"

"When the professor withdrew his offer, the owner did some serious negotiating. When he got down to $10,000, our philanthropic publisher here put up the money—in exchange for the story rights, of course."

The editor flipped through his pad.

"Well, I guess that's it!" Simpson said. "Oh, one other thing—when the thieves were caught, didn't one of them claim he had the scroll?"

"The thief you're speaking of is the one who was the laborer at the excavation site. He claimed he had grabbed the scroll when he ran . . . said he threw it in a dry creek behind the house."

"But it wasn't found, right?" Simpson asked.

"That's right," Jim answered. "The army searched pretty thoroughly, but they didn't find a thing."

"Do you believe his story?" Alex asked.

Jim shrugged his shoulders. "I *believe*," Jim said, standing up, "that it's time for me to catch my flight. Can you give me a lift, Alex?"

"Sure, but are you certain this is what you want to do?"

"I've never been more certain of anything in my life, Alex. I need to resolve some personal issues . . . some . . ." he stumbled on the words, "some spiritual issues. And until I do that, I don't intend to do anything else."

Alex nodded, and he put his hand on Jim's shoulders as they walked out of the office for the drive to the airport.

Halfway around the world, Abdul Ibn-Taleb grumbled at his stubborn donkey as they passed En-gedi on the shore of the Dead Sea. The afternoon sun sparkled on the placid water. Abdul shaded his eyes as he checked the angle of the sun. In less than an hour he figured the sun would drop below the yellow cliffs to grant him some relief from the heat. He didn't know it, but Joshua had rested in that exact same place after defeating the Canaanites. He didn't know that David had hid from Saul in a cave nearby or that John the Baptist once had preached there. Abdul knew nothing of this—he was only aware of selling his goods; he carried needles, thread, kerosene, matches, a few pots and pans, some dry-cell batteries . . . and one very old scroll.

# Other Living Books Bestsellers

**THE BEST CHRISTMAS PAGEANT EVER** by Barbara Robinson. A delightfully wild and funny story about what can happen to a Christmas program when the "horrible Herdman" family of brothers and sisters are miscast in the roles of the Christmas story characters from the Bible. 07–0137 $2.50.

**ELIJAH** by William H. Stephens. He was a rough-hewn farmer who strolled onto the stage of history to deliver warnings to Ahab the king and to defy Jezebel the queen. A powerful biblical novel you will never forget. 07–4023 $3.50.

**THE TOTAL MAN** by Dan Benson. A practical guide on how to gain confidence and fulfillment. Covering areas such as budgeting of time, money matters, and marital relationships. 07–7289 $3.50.

**HOW TO HAVE ALL THE TIME YOU NEED EVERY DAY** by Pat King. Drawing from her own and other women's experiences as well as from the Bible and the research of time experts, Pat has written a warm and personal book for every Christian woman. 07–1529 $2.95.

**IT'S INCREDIBLE** by Ann Kiemel. "It's incredible" is what some people say when a slim young woman says, "Hi, I'm Ann," and starts talking about love and good and beauty. As Ann tells about a Jesus who can make all the difference in their lives, some call that incredible, and turn away. Others become miracles themselves, agreeing with Ann that it's incredible. 07–1818 $2.50.

**EVERGREEN CASTLES** by Laurie Clifford. A heartwarming story about the growing pains of five children whose hilarious adventures teach them unforgettable lessons about love and forgiveness, life and death. Delightful reading for all ages. 07–0779 $3.50.

**JOHN, SON OF THUNDER** by Ellen Gunderson Traylor. Travel with John down the desert paths, through the courts of the Holy City, and to the foot of the cross. Journey with him from his luxury as a privileged son of Israel to the bitter hardship of his exile on Patmos. This is a saga of adventure, romance, and discovery — of a man bigger than life — the disciple "whom Jesus loved." 07–1903 $3.95.

**WHAT'S IN A NAME?** compiled by Linda Francis, John Hartzel, and Al Palmquist. A fascinating name dictionary that features the literal meaning of people's first names, the character quality implied by the name, and an applicable Scripture verse for each name listed. Ideal for expectant parents! 07–7935 $2.95.

# Other Living Books Bestsellers

**THE MAN WHO COULD DO NO WRONG** by Charles E. Blair with John and Elizabeth Sherrill. He built one of the largest churches in America . . . then he made a mistake. This is the incredible story of Pastor Charles E. Blair, accused of massive fraud. A book "for error-prone people in search of the Christian's secret for handling mistakes." 07–4002 $3.50.

**GIVERS, TAKERS AND OTHER KINDS OF LOVERS** by Josh McDowell. This book bypasses vague generalities about love and sex and gets right down to basic questions: Whatever happened to sexual freedom? What's true love like? What is your most important sex organ? Do men respond differently than women? If you're looking for straight answers about God's plan for love and sexuality then this book was written for you. 07–1031 $2.50.

**MORE THAN A CARPENTER** by Josh McDowell. This best selling author thought Christians must be "out of their minds." He put them down. He argued against their faith. But eventually he saw that his arguments wouldn't stand up. In this book, Josh focuses upon the person who changed his life — Jesus Christ. 07–4552 $2.50.

**HIND'S FEET ON HIGH PLACES** by Hannah Hurnard. A classic allegory which has sold more than a million copies! 07–1429 $3.50.

**THE CATCH ME KILLER** by Bob Erler with John Souter. Golden gloves, black belt, green beret, silver badge. Supercop Bob Erler had earned the colors of manhood. Now can he survive prison life? An incredible true story of forgiveness and hope. 07–0214 $3.50.

**WHAT WIVES WISH THEIR HUSBANDS KNEW ABOUT WOMEN** by Dr. James Dobson. By the best selling author of *DARE TO DISCIPLINE* and *THE STRONG-WILLED CHILD*, here's a vital book that speaks to the unique emotional needs and aspirations of today's woman. An immensely practical, interesting guide. 07–7896 $2.95.

**PONTIUS PILATE** by Dr. Paul Maier. This fascinating novel is about one of the most famous Romans in history — the man who declared Jesus innocent but who nevertheless sent him to the cross. This powerful biblical novel gives you a unique insight into the life and death of Jesus. 07–4852 $3.95.

**BROTHER OF THE BRIDE** by Donita Dyer. This exciting sequel to *THE BRIDE'S ESCAPE* tells of the faith of a proud, intelligent Armenian family whose Christian heritage stretched back for centuries. A story of suffering, separation, valor, victory, and reunion. 07–0179 $2.95.

**LIFE IS TREMENDOUS** by Charlie Jones. Believing that enthusiasm makes the difference, Jones shows how anyone can be happy, involved, relevant, productive, healthy, and secure in the midst of a high-pressure, commercialized, automated society. 07–2184 $2.50.

**HOW TO BE HAPPY THOUGH MARRIED** by Dr. Tim LaHaye. One of America's most successful marriage counselors gives practical, proven advice for marital happiness. 07–1499 $2.95.

# Other Living Books Bestsellers

**DAVID AND BATHSHEBA** by Roberta Kells Dorr. Was Bathsheba an innocent country girl or a scheming adulteress? What was King David really like? Solomon — the wisest man in the world — was to be king, but could he survive his brothers' intrigues? Here is an epic love story which comes radiantly alive through the art of a fine storyteller. 07–0618 $3.95.

**TOO MEAN TO DIE** by Nick Pirovolos with William Proctor. In this action-packed story, Nick the Greek tells how he grew from a scrappy immigrant boy to a fearless underworld criminal. Finally caught, he was imprisoned. But something remarkable happened and he was set free — truly set free! 07–7283 $3.50.

**FOR WOMEN ONLY.** This bestseller gives a balanced, entertaining, diversified treatment of all aspects of womanhood. Edited by Evelyn and J. Allan Petersen, founder of Family Concern. 07–0897 $3.50.

**FOR MEN ONLY.** Edited by J. Allan Petersen, this book gives solid advice on how men can cope with the tremendous pressures they face every day as fathers, husbands, workers. 07–0892 $3.50.

**ROCK.** What is rock music really doing to you? Bob Larson presents a well-researched and penetrating look at today's rock music and rock performers. What are lyrics really saying? Who are the top performers and what are their life-styles? 07–5686 $2.95.

**THE ALCOHOL TRAP** by Fred Foster. A successful film executive was about to lose everything — his family's vacation home, his house in New Jersey, his reputation in the film industry, his wife. This is an emotion-packed story of hope and encouragement, offering valuable insights into the troubled world of high pressure living and alcoholism. 07–0078 $2.95.

**LET ME BE A WOMAN.** Best selling author Elisabeth Elliot (author of *THROUGH GATES OF SPLENDOR*) presents her profound and unique perspective on womanhood. This is a significant book on a continuing controversial subject. 07–2162 $2.95.

**WE'RE IN THE ARMY NOW** by Imeldia Morris Eller. Five children become their older brother's "army" as they work together to keep their family intact during a time of crisis for their mother. 07–7862 $2.95.

**WILD CHILD** by Mari Hanes. A heartrending story of a young boy who was abandoned and struggled alone for survival. You will be moved as you read how one woman's love tames this boy who was more animal than human. 07–8224 $2.95.

**THE SURGEON'S FAMILY** by David Hernandez with Carole Gift Page. This is an incredible three-generation story of a family that has faced danger and death — and has survived. Walking dead-end streets of violence and poverty, often seemingly without hope, the family of David Hernandez has struggled to find a new kind of life. 07–6684 $2.95.

The books listed are available at your bookstore. If
unavailable, send check with order to cover retail price
plus 10% for postage and handling to:

Tyndale House Publishers, Inc.
Box 80
Wheaton, Illinois 60189

Prices and availability subject to change without notice.
Allow 4–6 weeks for delivery.